# World Revolver

Gina Ranalli

*World Revolver*
Bloo Skize Dark
ISBN-13: 978-0692680711
ISBN-10: 0692680713

# World Revolver

*Don't eat animals.*

*Recycle.*

*Drive an eco-friendly car. Or better yet, don't drive at all. Walk. Or bike.*

*Leave only footprints.*

*These were, quite literally, the signs of the time, once upon a time.*

*Not so long ago either.*

*We could remember those signs, that time, if we really wanted to. But we don't. Of course we don't. If we think about it too much we'll realize, consciously, right up in our faces, how avoidable all this was. All the disasters. The starvations. The complete and utter ruin of our oceans, our planet and everything on it, including ourselves.*

*We weren't ignorant. We were selfish. We knew the score. Knew we were leaving the world unsustainable for our children. We didn't care. We covered our ears and hummed as loudly as we could. We thought the momentary pleasure of our taste buds was far more important. The only thing that mattered.*

*We said*

*-Don't preach to us. Get off your high horse. Tell it to someone who cares.*

*Some of us cared, but the problems were so big, so insurmountable that, what could we do? Get our share, that's what. Get as fat as we could, as fast as we could. Become hoarders of everything and in more quantity than we could ever need.*

*You get yours, I'll get mine and god help anyone who tries to take it from us, regardless of whether they need it more than we do or not.*

*And then we finally got what was coming to us: a whole lot of nothing. The planet just gave up the ghost. She's not gone yet, but her bags are packed and she's waving goodbye from the taxicab.*

*We are now on our own, wandering the corpse of our mother, and the strangest part is we still haven't really learned our lesson.*

# CHAPTER ONE—The Junkie (1)

We call the needle a rocket because it shoots you into space. If it's sucking out your life juice, then it's called a drain but that doesn't happen much. Not to me. I can't even remember the last time someone took my blood.

I wouldn't even call it a rocket if it was up to me. I'd call it a fang. A snake fang that pours its sweet venom into your veins and makes you go away for a while. Leave the shithole planet behind. Bliss out, far out.

Going away is my favorite thing to do. The only thing that matters in my shitty little life. Everything else can go fuck itself with a broken beer bottle for all I care. There's not a whole lot else to live for anyway. Not anymore.

I want the fang—the bitch's tooth—in my arm and I tell Harvey as much from my place on the mattress in the corner of the room. The mattress is on the floor—fuck box springs, who needs 'em—under the one window and next to a cranky old radiator. Outside, it's gray early afternoon and I live in this room alone. There's a refrigerator, a sink and a stove. This place was old before my mother was born. There's also a bathroom, painted infection pink, but no shower. Just a toilet and a tub. I have to brush my teeth in the main room.

Harvey's name isn't really Harvey but it amuses me to call him that because his last name is Dent and, being a dealer, he's naturally pretty sketchy and his face, though not completely mangled on one side, is pretty pock-marked all over. He wears suits a lot. Not nice ones, but suits just the same. Not sure why he bothers, really, but I give him credit for trying. I don't even own a suit. I used to, when I was a kid—I got it for my dad's funeral—but now all I have are t-shirts and sweats. One pair of jeans that still fit. Everything else is too big for me now. Not that I give a shit. I don't really go out that much these days anyway.

-Harvey, you gonna give me the shit or not?

-This is not your daddy's juice, bro.

Harvey likes to call me bro. he waves the syringe in the air, trying to tempt me with it like he's a seductive woman looking all come hither. But he knows he doesn't have to tempt me. I already want it.

He's leaning against the wall by the door, his striped tie loose around his neck and his brown shoes scuffed, giving away his real status in life.

-Harvey, man—

-Why the fuck do you keep calling me that? I told you a million fucking times it's not funny.

-Okay. Sorry.

-You think you're being original with that shit? Like I haven't heard it my whole fucking life?

-I said sorry, man.

Harvey stares at me like I'm a maggot on his French toast.

-This shit is different. And it's gonna cost you. We're not playing anymore, Jeffy.

-Yeah, you told me. How much?

-Two bens, baby.

-What the fuck?

Harvey shrugs, like he just works in the store, he doesn't own it. I guess that might be true but it's still weird to think about.

I dig out my wallet, find the money.

-This better be worth it.

-It is. But you gotta be careful. This is gonna fuck up

your mind beyond belief. It could be the best high of your life or it could be the worst. Like that retard Gump said, you never know what you're gonna get.

-That doesn't sound worth it to me.

-What? You want references? I can get you references. Trust me, Jeffy. If you get a good one, it's worth double the price. You'll see. It's a fucking steal.

I lick my lips. I've heard about the shit. Satellite, it's called. Supposed to send you to another plane of existence. Another dimension. Fucking crazy talk, you ask me, but what the hell. I'll try anything once and if it's as good as I've heard, it'll be unlike anything else. Sounds better than just nodding out, as good as that can be.

-You gotta be careful. It's like a dream, Jeffy. You die in the dream, you ain't waking up back here. You get what I'm saying?

-Bullshit.

I have to laugh but Harvey walks over and swaps me, money for needle. He isn't smiling.

-You think I'm kidding? I'm not fucking kidding. You go, you're stuck there till this shit wears off. Then you're back here, all comfy in your fucking palace.

He looks around the room and snorts sarcastically.

-Okay. You're not fucking kidding. Got it.

-I'll be back tomorrow. You'll either be dead or you'll want more.

-Isn't that how it always is?

-Yeah, but usually you can afford it. This is gonna add up, bro. Fast.

I make a gun out of my finger and thumb and shoot him with it.

-Gotcha.

Harvey leaves and I'm alone with the rocket and my thoughts. The radiator hisses for a while. I wonder if I'm gonna have to resort to sucking cock if I like this shit. Wouldn't be the first time. I've done it before and it doesn't mean I'm queer. It means I'm skilled. A man does what he has to do to get by in life. That's what my dad told me and I believe him. You might not like it, but tough shit. Nobody likes their job. My dad told me that too.

But first things first. Not gonna worry about cash until I know this shit is worth it. Forgive me for not just taking Harvey's word for it. Or anyone else's. I like to find this shit out for myself. Besides, my mom is usually good for a few bens now and then. Fuck, she usually pays my rent and then some. Otherwise, things have a way of working out. Never underestimate the power of shit jobs under the table. Hell, my landlord will give me shit to do around the building if I ask him. Knock a few bills off the bill, you know?

I get up off the mattress. There's some shit I like to do every time before I get high. Call it experience.

First things first.

Gotta piss. Shit if you can, but if you can't, fuck it. Next, grab a bottle of water, put it within arm's reach because when you come back, you're gonna be dehydrated like a motherfucker. I like to take my driver's license out of my wallet and put it nearby, make it really obvious. You never know who might find you and if you don't came back, you want them to know who you are, no mistakes. Unless you don't. I shouldn't assume. But that's what I do.

Piss.

Check.

Water.

Check.

ID.

Check.

And I don't have to tell you about the tourniquet. That one even my grandmother would know, if she wasn't already dead like the rest of everybody I was ever related to. Except mom, that is.

With Satellite, there's no cooking. No mess. No fuss. Or whatever that expression is. Just let that fang bite you and you're on the way, which is pretty sweet. Not a lot a person could fuck up. Not even me, the biggest royal fuck-up you'd ever not wanna meet.

Back to the mattress, all the arrangements made. I'm ready for my ride.

It's 2 PM, Wednesday afternoon, September 25, 2036.

Let's go.

## CHAPTER TWO—The Rock Star

What can I say, I'm a spoiled motherfucker.

The bitch going down on me is doing it for free and I can't argue with that. Hell, I think she would have paid me for the honor. Sometimes I'm tempted to ask the women just that, but you know, I have to be a gentleman. To some degree anyway.

Stretched out on my California King, my bedroom decorated in royal purple, blood red and jet fucking black, I let her do her thing and watch the shadows on the silver ceiling, half wondering what's going on downstairs. Candles burn throughout the room and I like the effect. Chicks seem to dig it too. Or, it's just me they dig. Who I am, what I have, who I might introduce them to. All that shit. They dig the stuff a lot though. All the stupid shit I have hanging around. The guitars, the Grammy, the clothes and jewelry, the gold records. Not to mention the crap that only money can buy, like the tiny fucking shirt Cobain wore in the "Smells Like Teen Spirit" video, one of Hunter S. Thompson's typewriters, a painting done by the old dharma bum himself, Kerouac. Another one by John Wayne Gacy that hangs in the kitchen—one of his many clowns. Collectable crap like that. You have to be rich to be able to afford things that belonged to your heroes, especially when they're everybody else's heroes too.

The girl—I think she said her name was Violet, but she said it weird, like it's probably not her real name— takes care of business and then crawls up my body, trying to kiss me on the mouth.

-Nope, I don't do cum, sweetheart. There's new toothbrushes in the bathroom. Go use one.

She gives me an insulted look but says nothing, taking her sweet bare ass out of my bed and away.

Poof. I wave at her ass like a magician, a fancy finger motion, making her go bye-bye.

Once she's disappeared, I sit up and light a smoke, one of the few vices besides the chicks I'm still allowed. No more drugs, no more booze. Thanks Mr. Manager, ya fucking prick. Said my career would be down the shitter if I kept up my so-called hard living, whatever the fuck that means. A few too many busts, a few too many punches at the fucking paparazzi and way too many moving violations. Two stints in rehab, which the media ate like cum-covered ice cream, the fuckers. Nothing like a rock star going down in flames to start a feeding frenzy amongst the vultures.

I smoke and listen to the water running in the bathroom and hope no one downstairs is fucking anything up. The usual hangers-on tagged along after the show earlier tonight, a few guys from the band and the female stragglers who follow us like they're puppies and we have pockets full of bacon. A couple of the tech guys too. I don't know them too well, so I should probably head down there and make sure they aren't touching shit they shouldn't touch or whatever. Wouldn't be the first time I had strangers in my house who ripped me off. Usually they steal stupid shit, like clothes or other personal items, so they can sell them on auction sites.

The chick emerges from the bathroom wearing nothing but a sexy smile and I have to admit, she's a step up from the usuals. Doesn't look as strung out or desperate or, thank Christ, young.

She starts to crawl back into bed with me and I need

to nip that shit in the bud.

-Hold up. We're going back downstairs now.

-What? No cuddling?

I laugh and stab the cigarette out in an ashtray of James Dean's face.

-Not tonight, sweetheart.

-Later?

-I have shit to do. Gotta get back to my guests.

-I'm one of your guests.

-And you got the best treatment of all, cupcake.

-Oh, so it's like that?

I ignore her, get out of bed and put my jeans on.

-I suck your dick and get nothing in return? You can't even finger me?

She has a point, I guess, but I'm already feeling pretty tired.

-Rain check on that, okay, sweetheart?

-You don't even remember my name, do you? That's why you keep calling me sweetheart and cupcake, right?

Pulling a black silk shirt out the of the closet, I keep my back to her, hoping this doesn't turn into a fucking scene. I'm in no mood for a fucking scene.

I put the shirt on but don't bother buttoning it and face her.

-Don't be like that, Violet.

Her face, which was getting that long, grim look that older, angry women wear constantly, softened and she smiled again.

-I think you might really like me.

-That right?

I grab my smokes from the nightstand and head out of the room, not waiting for an answer. I hope I don't have to frisk the bitch before she leaves. Wouldn't be the first time for that one either. Love and war though, right?

Downstairs, Joey, my bass player, is wrestling with my only true friend in the world, Marvin, my boxer. Boxer like the dog, not the shitheads who pound each other stupid in a ring like fucking Neanderthals.

Marvin leaps up at the sight of me and races over, his stump of a tail wagging. I crouch and let him slobber my face with pup kisses.

Joey stands up and tries to act cool, with his black eyeliner and black polished fingernails. Goth went out in the '20s but joey doesn't let that stop him. I can't say too much about it though, given my own fondness for what they used to call grunge. You wouldn't know it to look at me but nothing sends me over the moon like those old tunes, full of angst and sweat.

-Where's everybody?

He gestures towards the sliding glass doors leading out to the patio.

-Pool.

-Not you though?

-Man, you know I can't swim. Plus, they're all…

-They're all what?

-Naked and shit.

-So?

-That's not fucking sanitary, man.

He shakes his mop head at me and clucks his tongue like somebody's damn grandma.

My man Marvin would just keep licking all night if I let him, so I give him a little push and straighten up, doing my best not to show my amusement at Joey being a fucking weirdo.

-I'm hungry.

I rub my belly when it growls and wander away into the kitchen to forage for food. I still have my head in the fridge when Violet's voice gets my attention. I seriously hope she's not planning on staying the night. I hate to seem like a douche bag, but shit.

-You gonna make me a meal in exchange for the b.j.?

I close the fridge and look at her. She's dressed now, if you can call it that. Skimpy outfit that leaves nothing to the imagination. I liked it when I first saw her but now it just makes me tired. *More* tired.

-I can't cook. Sorry.

-You want me to make you something?

Stifling a sigh, I scratch at my ear and look at the floor.

-It's late.

-You kicking me out?

I look up at her and don't say anything, hoping she'll take a hint. Well, a *bigger* hint.

-I read in a magazine you like breakfast food. I can make you an omelet if you want. Or pancakes.

The desperation wafting off her is practically visible, like a heat shimmer.

-I forgot to take a piss.

I leave the kitchen then, heading into the bathroom just off it, and when I'm done, I stand at the sink washing my hands, checking myself out in the mirror.

What I see, for the first time, probably, is a ridiculous man. I still have the same long crazy hair I had when I was in high school. Still too skinny. I look like a fucking junkie with sallow skin and sunken eyes who—

-The fuck?

There's a scar by my right eye, right at the outside corner, about an inch and a half long, faded, like it's many years old, but plenty visible.

It wasn't there before. Ever.

Leaning in close to the mirror, I touch the scar, can feel the slightly raised ragged line of it with the tip of my finger.

I get a funny feeling in my stomach, kind of nauseous, and it suddenly feels like my blood is itchy in my veins. What the fuck is going on?

The scar clearly came from a deep wound, but…

This shit makes no sense.

I stare at myself, at the scar, for a long time. I might have stayed there even longer, but Marvin starts scratching at the door and I blink, startled, and look away from the mirror. When I look back, the scar is gone. Totally gone.

Of course it's fucking gone. It was never there in the first place. I never cut my face, not even when I was a kid. No falling off a skateboard or hitting a windshield or getting nailed with a pop fly lost in the sun.

I grip the edges of the sink and continue to stare at myself. The same phrase—*what the fuck?*—runs over and over in my mind, like it's the only English I know.

A drug flashback? A premonition? What the fuck is wrong with me?

A trick of the light, I decide. It's the only thing that makes sense.

The sound of Marvin whining at the door distracts me again and when I open it, the scent of cooking food assaults my nostrils. Is that chick actually making me breakfast at midnight? Maybe I shouldn't kick her out just yet.

Marvin pushes past me into the bathroom and proceeds to help himself to a nice fresh bowl of toilet water.

-Nasty ass dog.

I give myself one last glance in the mirror and then get the fuck out of there. I don't know what that little hallucination was about and I really don't want to. For all I know, it could be a newborn brain tumor bursting from my frontal lobe like a huge zit getting ready to pop. Or it could be the first sign of schizophrenia or Alzheimer's and I'll be drooling in a corner by the end of the year.

In the kitchen, Violet is at the stove and the smell of bacon is growing. Joey is seated at the table and a few of the others are mingling about, cluttering up my house and my peace, my sanctuary.

Rick, my drummer, has a blonde hanging off his shoulder and they're both looking a little green around the gills.

-You okay, man?

He smiles at me and then I know the fucker has been shooting up in my backyard.

-Okay, you know what? Everybody, get the fuck out. Party is fucking over.

Joey immediately gets to his feet. He knows me better than anyone else and he knows when I'm not fucking around.

In less than two minutes, everyone is gone, ushered from the backyard, through the house and out the front door, except for Violet, who apparently has pretended she didn't hear the command or she thinks she's exempt from it.

I'm sitting where Joey was and watching her move around the kitchen, searching for shit like salt and plates and mugs. I can't believe the balls on this one. Does she think sucking my dick is the same as an engagement ring?

Fuck it.

I let her cook for me, feed me, talk to me about her life, but I don't really listen all that much. Eventually, I travel into the living room and sprawl out on the crushed velvet sectional sofa with my old Ovation and strum the first few chords of a song called "Cash Kills," something that was a hit a long time ago by a band no one remembers anymore.

Violet stays in the kitchen for a long time, loading the dishwasher and doing whatever the fuck she's doing in there and I'm yawning, playing songs without singing them, but every couple minutes I flash back to that weird experience in the bathroom.

When Violet finally finishes cleaning up, she joins me on the couch and listens to me play for a few minutes.

-Pretty. You should play on stage more often.

I nod.

-Yeah, I should. But I'm not that good, really. Joey and Chris are the real musicians.

-I doubt that.

She moves closer to me, pressing herself into my body, and starts rubbing my crotch. My dick surprises me by responding instantly and I set aside the guitar and dig my hands into her hair.

I think I'll fuck her this time. Show her the tabloids are right about my stamina and all the other bullshit they've been writing for years.

Deep inside her, listening to her moan, a new song begins to form in my head, something about movement, time…life and circles, always evolving.

Revolving.

## CHAPTER THREE—The Junkie (2)

I come back, sit straight up and puke all over my lap.

*What the fuck was that?*

The queasiness passes almost immediately, but my pulse is racing like a terrified little bird suddenly trapped in a cage made out of razors.

Not giving a shit that I'm covered in vomit, I lie back again, staring at the water stained, cracked gray ceiling. It takes me a moment to realize my dick is hard, something it hasn't been in I don't know how long.

It seems like a good sign. A bonus side effect.

I've never in my life felt a high like the one I've just experienced. And I've had a lot of highs, both good and bad. But this one…holy shit. Fucking amazing and I know one thing surer than I've ever known anything: I need more. I need to do it again. It's what I've been searching for my whole life-the greatest escape of all.

I try to remember every moment of the trip. I was a fucking *rock star*! A rich, famous fucking rock star, surrounded by drugs which for some reason I wasn't into but whatever—and at least one chick begging for my cock. Probably with plenty more where she came from. A kick-ass dog, friends, expensive shit in an expensive house, the whole fucking nine. Everything I could want. Hell, I could play guitar, something I've wanted to learn to do my entire life but could never seem to work up the needed discipline.

It was *me*. I was him. The scar was the clincher. I reach up and touch it. Though it had mystified my other self, I knew exactly how I'd gotten it and when. A broken glass bottle thrown at my face when I was nine and trying to steal a pair of sneakers off another kid's feet. His dad, a grizzled, wino-looking dude, hadn't taken too kindly to it and whipped the nearest object at my head while screaming that he was gonna cut my balls off and feed em to a pack of wild dogs.

I wasn't nearly quick enough and caught the bottle in the temple where it split the side of my eye wide open. I'd always considered myself lucky that I hadn't lost the eye. A quarter of an inch to the left and I would have.

I don't know why that other drug-induced version of me didn't have it. I know even less why he then *did* have it, and then didn't again, but maybe drug-induced me never had to steal anything. Drug-induced me seemed to have a pretty cushy fucking gig.

But what did it mean? Could I become that guy? Have that cushy rock star life?

The idea makes me laugh aloud. Of course fucking not. No way. But I *want* that life now. More than anything. And if that means I have to stay high forever, then so be it. I can do that, no problem. I won't be missing anything here, that's for fucking sure.

I just need to get more. Find Harvey. Beg, borrow, steal, whatever.

But finding Harvey in the first place—if I even can—means I have to go out into the world, which sucks balls. But, fuck it. It'll be worth it.

First things first.

Get up, take a goddamn bath, wash this puke off me. Spit and polish, like they used to say back in the day.

Running the dirty brown water into the tub takes longer than actually being in the tub and sitting in it is no picnic. It doesn't help that the claustrophobia-inducing bathroom's color reminds me of the inside of a migraine, so I'm in and out, barely using the same sliver of soap I've had for probably six months already.

I got wet. That's good enough for me.

Pulling on cleanish sweat pants and a new t-shirt, both of which I washed by hand in the sink a few days back, I'm pretty much ready to roll.

Stepping into shoes duct taped together at the toes, I grab my keychain with the one key on it and get going.

Night is falling and it's drizzling outside, as usual. And cold too. I don't put the temperature higher than 45 degrees or so, wishing like fuck I had a jacket. Or even a winter coat, if I want to really dream. I bet rock star me has a whole closet full of coats, probably a full-length fur or two included.

*That* Jeff is living the good life, man. And soon I will be too, if I have my way.

The streets are pretty much deserted. Nobody wants to come out in this crappy weather. Hell, they don't want to come out at all, if they can help it and I don't blame them. I'm the same way. This shit city is going south fast. No jobs to speak of, no nothing but empty buildings, some of which are about a season away from collapsing altogether.

I walk towards the west side, where a bar called Sennacherib's is still operational and the most likely place I can think of for Harvey to be.

It takes me twenty minutes to get there and by the time I arrive I'm wet, cold and cranky but thankful I didn't get jumped along the way.

I'm surprised to see about ten people inside, all men of course, but Harvey isn't among them.

The place is small and gloomy; it's hard to see the two guys in the back shooting pool. They're little more than shadows moving against the backdrop of a couple of dart boards and framed pictures of chicks in bikinis leaning over Corvettes and classic Mustangs.

I go up to the bar trying to shake the rain out of my hair. Hoop is here, like he always is. It's his place and has been in his family for three generations. Supposedly my dad drank with his dad and they went through some shit together but I have no idea if that's true or not. Old guys seem to love their tales of grandeur more than just about anything.

Hoop gives me a nod and I return it, slipping onto a stool.

-What's up, man?

He shrugs, his bald head gleaming, the brightest object in the whole place.

-Nada. You want a drink?

-On the house?

-Fuck you.

-For a price, doll face.

He gives me a disgusted look and starts to turn away from me.

-Whoa. Hold up. You seen Harvey?

-Who?

-Dent, I mean.

-Ah. Not yet. He'll be by though. He usually is.

-Soon?

-How the fuck should I know? It ain't my turn to babysit his ass.

I sigh and shiver and look at the guy a couple stools down who's eyeing me like he sees a steak.

-Spot me a brew, man?

The guy is older, a grayhead, with deep creases all over his face and a craggy beard.

-What's in it for me?

-Stimulating conversation?

He grunts and looks away.

-I'm just kidding, man. What do you want?

Again, that look. He definitely sees something edible but I'm crossing my fingers it isn't a literal thing. Cannibalism is more common than it used to be. Not a thing you hear about every day, but it's getting to be once a month maybe. Seriously fucked up shit. People have fallen on some hard fucking times.

-What's your name, kid?

-Jeff. What's yours?

He thrusts out a gnarled hand across the gulf of the two stools between us. "Halleck. Richard Halleck the third."

-No shit?

I shake his hand and try to look impressed but I have no fucking clue who he is and I'm not even sure he expects me to.

-No shit. Hoop, give this kid a drink on me. He looks like he could use it.

Hoop does as he's told without a word and then goes back to ignoring his customers, his concentration on a decaying old titty magazine.

-Thanks, Richard Halleck the third. You're a scholar and a gentleman.

I'm taking my first sip of the vaguely coolish beer when Harvey walks in out of the sad sack of a night.

-Yo, bro.

I beat him to his bro and he looks surprised.

-Eon. What a fucking surprise.

Halleck gives me an untrusting look.

-I thought you said your name was Jeff?

-It is. Jeff Eon.

He eyes Harvey, sizing up the competition maybe.

Harvey sits between us.

-Looking for me?

-How'd you guess?

-I'm fucking psychic. I warned you, didn't I? Just once and you're hooked.

Hoop looks up from his magazine, gives us a dirty look. He has rules. No drugs in his bar. Not because he's morally opposed or thinks he'll get raided or anything like that but because he says if people are high on other shit, they're less likely to have cash for booze or even want booze if they have cash. Catch 22, he always says, though I don't think the analogy applies like he thinks it does.

-Head outside for a minute?

-I just got here, motherfucker. Mind if I dry off before I start chasing your ass around?

I sigh but nod. You can't push Harvey to do anything he doesn't wanna do. If you try, he'll stonewall you hardcore.

He gets a drink from hoop, paying with cash— probably the same cash I gave him earlier—and sips it casually, pretending like he doesn't know me for a while.

Hoop walks to the other end of the bar and I clear my throat, talking soft.

-You need to hook me up, man.

-Can you pay for it?

I try to give him my best sorrowful puppy eyes.

-Then fuck yourself.

The Halleck guy leans towards Harvey.

-Give the kid what he wants. I'll cover him.

And I think, *oh fuck*.

Something tells me I'm gonna be paying dearly for whatever happens next and probably not in the way of an IOU either.

But I want it. Bad. Whatever the cost, I know it'll be worth it.

I look at my new beneficiary, if that's what he is, I look him square in the eye.

-Let's do it, old timer.

## CHAPTER FOUR—The Killer

The apartment complex is dark and quiet as I move through the parking lot. It's just after midnight and I know exactly where I'm going. To the newlyweds' place. Number A-4.

They've only lived here for a few months but I saw them moving in. They have a lot of nice shit. And a shiny new car too, that still had streamers and cans tied to the back bumper and the words 'just married' painted across their back windshield in soap.

They're young. Younger than me for sure. And happier than me too. I don't know what they do for work, but they're fairing pretty good, especially compared to everyone I know. We're all just a bunch of lifetime fuck-ups with no prospects on the horizon.

I keep my eyes open for any movement as I climb the steps up to the newlyweds' door. Their car is gone, just like it is every Wednesday night. No clue where they go but it's good for me that they do.

Making friends with the woman who manages the complex was pretty smart, if I do say so myself. She has keys in the office—keys I helped myself to one night while she was outside talking to one of the tenants about a noise complaint. She didn't even notice. I made sure to only grab a couple at a time, make copies and return them the next night. The chick—Jamie is her name—is pretty sweet on me. She's one of those fat, insecure girls that'll take attention from wherever she can get it. Sad, really, but what I'm doing isn't hurting her any. I get to let myself into people's apartments and she gets to think a young, handsome-ish guy is into her. Boost her ego while I boost my wallet.

The cops have been by every time I've broken into a place, though usually not until the next day. Three times so far. So, yeah, they know something is up, as do all the tenants. They had a meeting and everything, which was kind of funny, since I was there, acting all appalled and concerned, just like everybody else. Even volunteered to do the "neighborhood watch", take a shift during the early morning hours of Saturday, since I'm up anyway.

At first I thought it would be perfect—break-in while I'm on watch, patrolling the grounds, supposedly, but after I thought about it, I decided that might make it obvious who was doing the crimes.

I've been pretty careful, fucking up locks when I can so no one figures out about the keys. I mean, they'll figure it out eventually, but I'll be long gone before they do. That is, if luck is on my side and I have no reason to think it won't be. It has been so far.

At the newlyweds' door, I turn and look around one last time to make sure I'm not being observed. I even check the windows of other apartments. Satisfied the coast is clear, I unlock the door and slip inside, closing it behind me, soft as a whisper in the dark.

They left a light on in the kitchen, the one above the stove, so it's dim inside, which is good. Just how I like it.

I slink around, taking the place in. It's nice. They have nice furniture and electronics and all that shit. I'm not really sure what I want. I never am and never go into a place with anything in particular in mind. Mostly small stuff is what I'm after. Jewelry, credit cards, any cash lying around. I'm sure as fuck not stupid enough to try walking out with a 65" plasma flat-screen TV, though it would sure as shit be nice. But I can't be overly ambitious—I live in the complex too, for the time being anyway. Gotta take it easy, not get greedy.

Checking out stuff on the counter in the kitchen, I examine a checkbook, debating on pocketing it when there's a squeak behind me, like a chirping little bird.

I turn slowly and just about shit my pants when I see the wife standing there in the doorway, dressed in flannel pajamas and holding a tissue to her nose. Her eyes are wide and frightened and the moment we make eye contact she spins on her bare feet and starts to run away down the hall.

-Fuck.

There's a moment when I think about just getting the fuck out of there, jumping in my car and taking off right away. No fuss, no muss. But then I'm chasing her. Out of fear or panic, I'm not sure which. Maybe both.

She's racing towards the bathroom, crossing the threshold into it and in the process of slamming the door when I hit it hard with my left shoulder, all my weight behind it. She flies backwards, lands on her ass and starts to scream. I'm on her before she can get out much sound, my fist colliding with her mouth, rocking her head back, knocking it hard into the tile floor. There's a moment when she's dazed, her eyes rolling back in her head, showing only the whites. Her bared teeth are smeared with blood from her split lower lip and a horrifying thought occurs to me. What if she's not alone here? What if her husband is home too? Maybe they let someone borrow their car.

Straddling her body, I look over my shoulder, half expecting to see an enraged man charging me with a steak knife aimed at my back, but there's nothing. No one. It's just me and her.

My heart in my throat, I start thinking about shit I

never thought about before. Things like fingerprints, shoe patterns, carpet fibers and DNA.

I'm already caught, I think. Already fucked forever. And it's this dumb bitch's fault. Why the fuck is she home? This could have been so easy. In and out like all the rest. No one had to get hurt. But here we fucking are, both of us fucked now. Both of us.

She starts wriggling beneath me and I almost hit her again but my knuckles are already sore and bleeding which brings me back to fucking DNA again. So instead of hitting her, I wrap my hands around her throat and squeeze as hard as I fucking can.

Her thrashing is so violent she almost jolts me off her body but I hold on like a cowboy riding a bucking bronco. Her eyes are wide open. *Wide* open. And I'm staring into them, pools of blue space holding me transfixed, mesmerized, almost the way it is when you're gazing into the eyes of someone you're in love with, long before they break your heart.

The whites of her eyes abruptly fill with blood. Something in them bursts, capillaries or something, and she stops flailing around as much, her movements becoming slow and sluggish until she's completely still, her focus remaining on me and I keep squeezing. Her neck is small. She's small, really. A petite thing and I'm reminded of a bird with their fragile bones, so easy to snap even if it's by accident.

I remember a parakeet. Blue and white, in its cage in the kitchen of the house where I grew up. Me, eight years old, trying to catch it in my fist, but it was scared and flying around inside the cage and by the time I'd caught it, I just squeezed too hard. I heard tiny twigs snap and then the bird was still. So easily, with no effort at all.

Just like this woman I'm on top of.

What a shitty way to end—or maybe begin—the night.

I have a headache all of a sudden and I crawl away from her body, eyeing the toilet, wondering if I'm gonna puke. I feel like I am. I lean my back against the wall, which feels impossibly cool and wonderful through my shirt. It gives me comfort and I swallow hard, trying to settle my shaking. It seems like it goes on for a long time and for a while not only am I in danger of throwing up but I'm also in danger of crying.

*Fuck.*

Why did this have to happen? Why couldn't she just have gone off with her tall, handsome husband like they did every other Wednesday night?

I notice the tissue still gripped in her hand.

Sick, probably. She'd been too sick to go out and now she was dead.

Life is unfair as a motherfucker.

My head still pounding, my stomach still roiling, I climb slowly to my feet. I need to get out of here. I don't know how much time has passed but it seems like a century. I feel like a different person and I suppose I am. I'm a killer now. A woman killer. The newlywed killer.

I wonder if that's what the media will name me. They love to give names to killers who piss people off more than just the average amount of pissed off. And I think this case might qualify.

Leaving the bathroom, I make my way into the bedroom, to the window, which looks down on the parking lot and the outside stairs leading up to the apartment. There's still no movement anywhere. The coast is clear once again. Or still. Whatever.

I slip out the door, using my shirt sleeve cuff on the knob, both inside and out. I'm still thinking about fingerprints and hoping I didn't leave any inside. I don't think I touched much. I was mostly still in the looking around phase but that fact doesn't give me much comfort.

Halfway across the parking lot, a car pulling into the complex. A yellow Volkswagen, one of my neighbors, and he looks right at me, even brakes his car a little when he sees me, and he waves.

I wave back and hurry away, my heart still lodged in my throat. I've been seen. He'll remember. He'll tell the cops when they come. I probably don't have much time. Hours at most. Maybe less, if the groom decides to call home to see how his sick bride is faring. Maybe he'll feel guilty about leaving her alone. And when she doesn't answer? Maybe he'll assume she's asleep, trying to recover. Maybe not.

All I know for sure is that I'm fucked. My life is over almost as permanently as hers is. As his is.

I wonder what my parents will think. My co-workers. Friends.

It feels like what I imagine having an out of body experience would feel like. A strange disconnect, like I'm not completely myself, and I think briefly of defense attorneys and bars of cold, hard steel.

My knuckles are still painful, bleeding, evidence.

I have to go now.

## CHAPTER FIVE—The Junkie (3)

I wake up in an armchair and I know immediately I'm not at home because I don't own an armchair.

My mouth is desert dry and the light in this room is dim and golden, like candlelight. The first thing I can really focus on is a wall of bookcases, filled to overflowing and made of some dark wood I can't identify.

-How was your trip?

I want to say terrible but I can't gather enough spit in my mouth to form any words. And there's the fact that I don't know who's speaking to me. Some guy I can't see.

There's a terrifying moment when I think maybe I've been kidnapped. Maybe I'm tied down. I try to raise my arm and it comes up easily, the relief washing over me like the cool water I wish I was drinking.

I touch my face, feel the roughness of my cheek. It's not unusual. I shave once a week if I'm feeling ambitious.

A man steps into my line of vision and he looks familiar. It's what's-his-name. From Sennacherib's.

Halleck.

He leans forward at the waist, peering into my face. When he reaches a hand towards me, I flinch away, but he grabs my head and uses his fingers to make my eye open wider, as if he's a doctor or something. He studies me for a few seconds, then releases me.

-What was it like?

I try to reply but only a croak comes out. I wish I knew what the fuck was going on. I'm suspicious he might have shoved his dick down my throat while I was out, causing it to be dry and sore. Fucker.

-It was a rough one by the look of it.

I want to tell him that, yeah, it was, but hey, at least I didn't puke on myself when I came back this time. That almost makes up for maybe being a murderer or whatever the fuck that was. Not really, but almost.

-How do you feel? What happened?

Getting to my feet, I push past him and look around. We're in a basement, but it's a nice one. Finished. The only reason I can even tell it's a basement is because the ceiling is so low and there are little rectangular windows right up close to it, too high to be able to see anything more than sky though.

There are wooden posts holding up the ceiling and off to one side there's one of those huge, old sinks, separated into two halves and almost deep enough to bathe in. I stumble over to the sink and turn on the faucet. I don't bother waiting to see if the water is clear or not—just stick my head under and drink deep. Lucky for me, the water seems fine. Better than fine. Right then it's probably the best thing I've ever swallowed in my whole life.

When I've had my fill, I turn off the faucet, wipe water from my chin and look back at Halleck still standing by the chair I was sitting in.

I'm surprised to see Hoop standing beside him, meaty arms folded across his barrel chest, glaring at me.

-What is this? An intervention?

The two men exchange a glance without humor and I immediately feel uneasy.

-Seriously. What the fuck is going on? Why am I here? And where is here, anyway?

Hoop unfolds his arms, then folds them again.

-Sit down, Eon.

He gestures at the chair with his chin.

I raise my voice a little louder.

-Where am I?

-In the basement of Sennacherib's. You're fine. We just want to talk to you.

-Is this about the no drugs in the bar thing? Because I don't remember coming here. All I remember is—

-It's not about that. It's about the drug itself. We want to know what you've been experiencing.

-Why?

They exchange another look and I'm becoming increasingly uncomfortable. Halleck steps forward a few paces.

-What did you see?

-I saw...I guess...I saw myself kill someone. A woman.

The sense of shame I feel saying it out loud is unexpected and overwhelming. I decide to take the offered seat after all. I'm queasy. Just like I was when I strangled the woman, felt her breathe her last breath.

But that wasn't me.

Was it?

-It wasn't *really* me. I was a rock star. That's what I wanted to get back to. That life. I was rich. I think I was pretty happy. But this time...I don't know. I don't know what that was about.

Halleck sits in a chair opposite me, leaning forward, elbows on knees.

-What was the world like?

I look at him.

-The world? What do you mean?

-Was it like this? Like our world? Or was it more futuristic? Was anything different?

-I...I don't know. I don't think so. Well, maybe a little

but I was inside for most of it.

Hoop makes an irritated groaning sound, like he's disgusted with my answer. Halleck ignores him.

-What did you see?

I shrug.

His eyes bore into me, making me more nervous still. I feel like I'm being interrogated when he repeats the question.

-*What did you see?*

-I don't know. Nothing, really. Just an apartment. An apartment complex. That's it.

-Was it nice?

-Yeah, I guess so.

-Where was it?

Stumped, I just stare at him.

-Was it here? This city?

Hoop, standing behind Halleck and a little to the right, puts a hand on the older man's shoulder.

-Never should have chosen him. I fucking told you.

This confuses me even further, not to mention worries me a bit.

-Chose me? For what?

I look around the basement again. There are not only books but mason jars on shelves against the wall opposite me. At first glance it looks like they might be filled with canned tomatoes—stewed I guess? Is that what they're called?—but then I realize whatever is in the jars looks too purple for tomatoes. This puzzles me but I look past them, past the men, and towards the stairs leading down here. I want to leave and wonder what would happen if I just got up and started to walk out. Would they stop me? Hurt me?

Then a good question occurs to me.

-Where's Harvey?

Halleck frowns.

-Who?

-Dent, I mean. Where's Dent?

-The guy with the rat face and the cheap suit? You don't need to worry about him. He's not involved with this.

-What exactly *is* this?

-We need to know what you saw when you crossed over.

-But Harvey told me—

Hoop takes a step closer to me, bringing him shoulder to shoulder with Halleck.

-Fuck Dent and fuck what he told you. He's just a parrot.

I'm liking this less and less. They're starting to act more like the mafia than cops and I'm hoping I don't give them a wrong answer but since I have no idea what's going on, it seems inevitable that I'll do just that.

Getting to my feet, I start walking towards the stairs. They both turn, watching me, and then Halleck grabs my arm. Not hard or threateningly but he grabs it just the same.

-I have what you want, Eon. Plenty of it. And if you want to go and live a happy life, I'm the only one who can make that happen for you.

I pull my arm free. I want to say something that makes me sound tough and unafraid, basically tell them to go fuck themselves, but the other part of me—the weaker, more desperate part—just wants more of the drug. Despite that last trip, if a trip is even what it was, the memory of living the good life is a fucking powerful one. Even if it's more like a dream than reality.

Halleck doesn't grab me again. He gestures at our surroundings, as if he's showing me around a palace.

-All you want. Within reason, of course. I'm not going to let you O.D. That would be terrible for business. But you need to tell us about your experiences. That's it.

I hesitate.

-So…let me get this straight. You'll get me high for…what exactly?

Halleck smiles then, his teeth yellow and a bit brown by the gum-line. Like everybody else's.

-Free.

-Free.

I don't ask, I just repeat.

-What's the catch?

-There's no catch, Eon. Nothing more than what I already told you. You go…visiting…and then report your findings. That's all.

-Visiting?

-Whatever you want to call it.

I look past him at Hoop, who's still staring at me like he's spotted shit on his shoe.

-What about you, Hoop? What about your no drug rule? This shit doesn't make any sense.

-The rules are the same as they've always been.

Hoop runs a hand over his bald head and maybe softens just a bit.

-Desperate times though, right?

-You're doing this for money?

-No, man. I'm doing it for the same reason you're going to do it.

-That right? What reason is that?

It seems to me like his eyes darken a shade before he replies but I'm sure that's just a trick of the light.

-A way out of this shithole place.

I nod like I understand but I really don't.

-So, why me then?

-You're the biggest junkie I know, man. Always have been. Even when we were kids, you were the one showing all the other kids how to huff shit or steal pills and crush 'em down to snort. You're like a fucking drug guru or something.

Despite everything, I laugh. Then I look at Halleck again.

-Free? Like, *totally* free? No strings? No catch?

Halleck sighs then, like he's getting bored with having to repeat himself. I can't really blame him but I want to be sure.

-No strings. Just talking.

I pull at the whiskers of my thin beard.

-Can I think about it?

Hoop is the one who laughs then.

-What for, man? You know you're just gonna say yes.

-How do you know?

-It's your nature.

There's not much about that I can argue with so I nod.

-When can I have more?

They look at each other and smile and I can't get rid of the nagging sensation that I may have just fucked myself worse than I ever have before. But there's something else too. A feeling that, no matter what these freaks have in mind, I'll soon be on top of the world and far away from here *and* them and there's nothing about that that sounds bad to me.

Hoop turns his pleased gaze to me.

-No time like the present, right, buddy?

# CHAPTER SIX—The Astronomer

The meteor shower is scheduled to start any minute and Jo isn't out here yet. I pop my head inside and call her name.

-Be right there.

The smell of popcorn wafts out to me and I can't help but smile. My kid knows how to have a good time—something me and Beth have tried to instill in her. Having a good time is the most important thing in life.

Well, that's my philosophy. Beth also tells Jo that being responsible and getting good grades is equally important and though I don't say anything, I secretly just want my kid to be happy, even more than responsible. I wouldn't say that out loud though. But Beth is a better parent than I am so I just defer to her wisdom in most things.

I go back to looking through the telescope and see the first shooting star. I call my daughter again, telling her to hurry up, she's missing it.

She emerges from the house a minute later, carrying the bowl of popcorn, Beth trailing after her.

-Wow, Dad. I just saw one and I'm not even looking through the telescope!

I look down at her and smile. She's only eight but her enthusiasm for the night sky is equal to my own. It's our thing and though Beth humors us and tries to play along, she's not all that interested. Not like Jo is.

-Pretty soon we might be able to see Venus.

-As long as it stays clear, right, Dad?

-Right.

I take the popcorn bowl from her and adjust the telescope so it's the right height for her, with a little help from a small step stool. She gets right to it, *ooing* and *ahhing* almost immediately.

Placing the bowl down on a table, I put an arm around my wife's waist and together we look up at the stars from our deck. It's such a beautiful night and there's just something about a meteor shower that always makes my blood feel electric somehow.

I'm living the life I'd always dreamed of—married my high school sweetheart, the only woman I've ever loved or ever cared to love and together we made this amazing, astounding little person who seems to me to be made of pure magic.

-Did you guys see that one?

Jo's voice is tinged with the excitement I feel myself and I use my free hand to ruffle the hair on her head.

-Sure did, kiddo.

Beth leans into me, her head on my shoulder.

-Wow. It's so clear out.

Jo laughs.

-So we can see the meteors!

-Right.

Jo and I stay out there for a couple hours while my wife goes back inside and cleans up the dinner dishes. It was supposed to be my turn but she's letting it slide this time.

Eventually Beth reappears in the doorway.

-Okay you two. It's getting late and it's a school night.

Jo groans with disappointment.

-But, *Mom.*

-No arguing. It's after nine. Come on in. Both of you.

Jo and I give each other sad looks but relent without further complaints. She races ahead and I grab the now empty popcorn bowl, carry it inside and close and lock the sliding glass door behind myself.

I look out one last time at the sky and see a bright blue light skimming just over the distant trees. Cocking my head, I frown, wondering what it is. A plane, I think, but then the light goes up, flying higher into the sky vertically. The speed with which it moved was astounding. I'm still staring when another blue orb joins the first one and they both proceed to do a kind of dance together, bobbing up and down like mating gnats.

-Beth?

I swallow hard and slide the door open again.

-Beth!

-Hold on, babe.

I barely hear her reply. I step back out onto the deck and the popcorn bowl slips from my fingers, clattering to the pine boards.

Bending over, I peer through the telescope, trying to get a fix on the flying objects but it's difficult. They're bobbing too fast, doing their strange dance around each other.

-What are they?

Jo's voice, from behind me, makes me jump.

-I'm not sure.

I try to keep my voice level but inside I'm buzzing with both excitement and fear.

-Go tell your mom to bring the video camera out, okay?

-I don't want to miss it!

-Just go tell her, honey.

She huffs a sigh and marches off and I go back to the telescope, wondering if I should call someone. But who? The police? Of course, they're probably already getting bombarded with calls so it might not be the best idea.

-Jeff?

I quickly glance over my shoulder at Beth and then point at the orbs. Her jaw falls open.

-Get the camera, okay, babe? I think this is important.

-What are they?

For some reason, I smile.

-I have no idea.

But I do have an idea. Of course I do. Anyone seeing the UFOs will have an idea.

Beth hurries away just as the objects get closer. Not close by any means but closer. I'd estimate they're still at least ten miles away. Assuming they're the size of an average airliner, which I suppose isn't that safe an assumption.

When Beth returns she has the camera, Jo trailing behind her. She's already recording what we see, Jo clinging to her leg, staring up at the sky with more wonder than I've ever seen on her face. She doesn't look frightened exactly, but not particularly excited either.

-I'm sure there's a good explanation for this.

The lights bob and dance, drawing closer still and then, like a lightning strike, a realization comes to me.

-Someone is watching.

-Huh?

Beth is still recording and doesn't glance at me. I don't glance at her either but I can't shake the feeling.

-Who's watching? The neighbors?

-No. someone else. From far away.

Now she does look over at me.

-Are you okay?

Slowly, I shake my head. I can't look away from the dancing lights now. I'm mesmerized and even though I'm completely aware of my surroundings, I suddenly feel as though I'm in a trance. My own voice sounds foreign to me.

-Who is that?

From the corner of my eye, I see Beth lower the camera, staring at me.

-Babe?

She touches my shoulder.

I repeat myself.

-*Who is that?*

-Who's what? In those things?

The lights continue to bob and dart in the night sky, the most beautiful blue I've ever laid eyes on. Like the irises of God.

-Something isn't right.

Beth, maybe unconsciously, takes a step forward, getting between Jo and the deck's railing.

-What's not right? You're starting to freak me out a little, hon.

I'm sweating, my palms damp, and I tip my head to one side, studying the nearing UFOs.

-Two of them?

An agonizing pain shoots through my skull and it takes everything I have to keep from screaming as I bend over clutching my head in both hands. I don't want to scare my daughter. I *cannot* scare my daughter.

-*Get her inside!*

Beth, trusting me in that amazing way she always has, doesn't question the command. She just takes Jo by the hand and they disappear into the house.

When I think they're a safe distance away, I cry out.

-*Who are you? What are you doing in there? Get out!*

I grip my hair in both fists and pull, for some reason thinking this will ease the pain that I'm positive is splitting my head in half from the inside.

It doesn't.

Falling to my knees, I look up and see the strange lights are closing the distance. They might be ten miles away now. Might be.

They're bigger than I had first thought. Much, much bigger.

-Please. You can't take my life.

And I'm sure that's what he—or they—want. They want my life. He's watching me now, so closely, with such a studious interest, desiring everything I have.

He means to replace me. I can feel his intent, almost hear his thoughts, which are so oddly similar to mine. It's almost my own voice in my head, but not quite.

Not quite.

-*I won't let you! Go away! Go the fuck away!*

-Jeff!

Beth is back, crouching on the deck beside me and I can feel him taking her in. Wanting her for his own.

The sweat is pouring off me now, soaking through my shirt, running in rivulets down my face and neck.

The next time I look up, the lights are nearly upon us and I realize...I realize...

-*Come on!*

Beth begins to drag me into the house, seizing one arm and pulling as hard as she can. She's so damn strong, my wife. So strong. Like our kid.

-*They're mine, you fucking bastard!*

From somewhere in the house, I can hear my daughter. She's crying now.

I'm crying too and fall down on the living room floor, still clutching my head.

The bastard is me.

## CHAPTER SEVEN—The Junkie (4)

I'm still in the basement and still not particularly happy about it. That last jaunt into Whereverland was a rough one—left me feeling rattled and exposed. Like a trespasser.

Halleck isn't around at the moment and Hoop is upstairs doing his barkeep thing. They say I'm not a prisoner but I sure as fuck feel like one.

When I told them what happened with the family man me, they both seemed fascinated, Halleck even took notes. They wanted to know every detail and I told them everything except one: Jo was my little sister's name. She was raped and murdered when we were kids. I was twelve and she was ten. I kind of always thought if I had a daughter—god fucking forbid—I'd name her Jo. But so far I've managed to not get caught in that particular prison—again, thank fucking god. I'm smart enough to wrap the rascal on the few occasions I do get lucky. The last thing I need is a brat running around or at the very least some woman nagging me for money because *she* has a brat running around. No thanks. Those of the snot-nosed variety are not for me.

But the whole thing gets me thinking. Did family man me have a sister too? He must have, right? I mean, he's me. And yet, he was so happy. He'd stayed in school, not dropped out at thirteen like I did, and then gone on to meet the love of his life. Would that have happened to me had I not let the death of my kid sister consume me? Would I have developed a love for the stars? For life?

He clearly had a good job, though I have no idea what

that might have been. Could I have found out though, had I been curious?

I think I could have.

And the blue lights? What were they? Aliens? Or am I the alien? The one he sensed watching him?

It seems more than likely. Probable, even.

This is so fucked up. I can't really wrap my head around it.

I need to get out of here. Get some fresh air. Maybe find Harvey and ask him what he really knows about all this shit, if anything. Maybe he really is, like Halleck said, just a parrot, telling *me* only what Halleck had told *him* about the drug. It seems out of character for Harvey though. The guy is a pain in the ass but not stupid. At least, I've never known him to be.

Climbing the stairs, I open the door at the top of them, entering the back room of Sennacherib's. There are cases of alcohol everywhere and it's more than tempting to help myself. I also have to wonder where Hoop is getting so much booze. It's not as attainable as it used to be.

I shrug these thoughts away, making a mental note to get back to them later. For now I just want out of here.

Poking my head into the bar area, I see the place is nearly deserted. Only one guy inside except for Hoop himself who, as usual, is busying himself with a dirty magazine.

There's no way I can walk out there without him noticing, so I decide to just do it and if he gives me any shit…well, I hope he doesn't. I'm not really the fighting type. Too skinny and not all that crazy about pain either.

I walk out, acting casual, like I'm not a prisoner at all. I have every right to leave the bar if I want.

Hoop looks up from his magazine just like I knew he

would.

-Going somewhere?

-Yeah. Anywhere but here. You gonna stop me?

-Nope.

He looks down at his magazine again, completely indifferent to me.

I hesitate.

-You're not? For real?

-I don't give a fuck what you do, Eon. But a word of advice. Be back tonight if you still want to continue your little trip fest. If not, we'll just find someone else. No skin off my dick.

Thinking about this for a moment, I stay right where I am. About fifteen feet away from the door and, potentially, freedom.

-I thought you guys wanted me specifically.

-You think you're special?

He laughs a little.

-Like there are no other junkies in the world? Are you shitting me?

The word junkie makes me bristle when he says it, even though I know good and goddamn well that's exactly what I am.

-Fuck you, Hoop.

I head for the door.

He chuckles again.

-Be back in time for dinner, sugar tits.

Ignoring him, I push open the door and step into the gray day. Afternoon, it turns out. Telling time in that dungeon of a basement is next to impossible, especially given the constant cloud cover and the fact that the windows only afford a view of the Northern sky and the lower half of people's legs as they pass by the bar on the sidewalk.

I start strolling in the direction of the rooming house, another headache teasing at my temples. I feel like shit again. Just drained. And I still have the thirst, whatever that's about. Tired, even though I haven't been up to anything particularly strenuous.

As usual, there aren't many people on the streets but I do pass by a pack of dogs surrounding a homeless dude sitting on the ground, his back against an old abandoned shop of some kind, now all boarded up and tagged with graffiti and crude drawings of tits and dicks.

-Change?

-Nope.

I keep walking, picking up the pace. I'm trying to decide if I even really want to go back to Sennacherib's or not. The trips are crazy. Good crazy or bad crazy—I don't know. And the whole being a guinea pig. Not sure how I feel about that either. Halleck hasn't told me shit. Why am I doing this? What's he getting out of it, besides the information he's always grilling me for? The whole thing is pretty fucking strange and I can't help but think it's probably dangerous somehow. It's gotta be, right? Or they'd be taking the shit themselves. Finding out what they want to know without some *junkie* having to relay everything and maybe not even coming back one night.

When I get to my building, I go inside and start fishing around in my pocket for the door key, climbing the stairs without really paying much attention to my surroundings, which isn't a good thing. I could get jumped for any number of reasons, none of them good.

Leaning against the wall beside my door is a chick I've never seen before. A tall blonde in black leather, from head to toe, looking as thin and dangerous as a razorblade.

-Eon.

It's not a question.

I look around, expecting some guy to leap out from somewhere while I'm being distracted by the blonde, but there's no one. It's just me and her in the hallway.

-Yeah?

She peels herself from the wall with the sound of crackling leather and offers me her hand.

-My name is Luna. I need to talk to you about what you've been doing.

I take the hand, surprised by how firm her shake is, but play dumb for all I'm worth. She doesn't look like any cop I've ever seen but I'm not taking any chances.

-What do you think I've been doing?

-You just came from Sennacherib's, didn't you?

Shifting my weight, I scratch my cheek.

-So?

-Can I come in?

-Uhhh…

-I think you'll be interested in what I have to tell you.

-And you can't do that out here?

-I'd prefer not to.

-Well…my place is a mess. And I don't have anything to offer you, except maybe a glass of water.

-That doesn't matter.

I'm not sure what to do. She's gorgeous, so one part of me is buzzing, but another part is smarter. More wary.

-Can you give me a hint what this is about?

-You're an intelligent guy. I'm sure you can figure it out.

This time I scratch my head.

-Are you a cop?

She smiles slightly, just one corner of her mouth rising a fraction.

-No.

-Promise?

Raising her right hand, three middle fingers up.

-Scout's honor.

I sigh, thinking this is so fucked up, then nod and unlock my door, holding it open for her.

She crosses the threshold and I follow, closing the door behind us, but not straying too far into the room. I want to be near the exit if anything weird starts to go down. What weird thing that might be, I have no idea but better safe than sorry, right?

After giving the room a quick once over, she turns to face me.

-Do you know what's going on?

-Uhhh...regarding what?

-You're being used, Eon.

-Oh. Yeah. Well, I figured that.

-The drug you've been taking is more than just a fun time. You also know that, I presume?

-Uh...uh huh. Figured that too.

-And do you know what it is? Exactly?

-A way to travel between dimensions?

She looks surprised, then nods.

-Precisely. And do you know why this is important?

I think about it, then shrug noncommittally.

-This is something we'll all have to do eventually, Eon. You're paving a highway. An inter-dimensional highway.

Pressing my lips together hard, I don't say anything. I have to keep from laughing.

She stares at me for a long moment.

-You don't believe me?

I change the subject.

-Okay. Who are you again? What do you have to do with this?

For the first time, this Luna woman seems a little

uncomfortable. Then:
    -I'm a spinner too.

## CHAPTER EIGHT—The Fisherman

Rowing back to the island with the paltry catch of the day at my feet, I look up at the foreboding sky. It's dark and already raining but I can tell a serious storm is on its way and I'd like to get off the water before the first lightning strikes.

In truth, I should have gone back to shore a good hour ago, but a grumbling stomach kept me out longer than I should have been. I like to eat once in a while and lately my diet has consisted of some stolen fruit and rice from the mainland and whatever my net can grab, which hasn't been much lately. Not to mention the fruit is gone and the rice is running low. I might be able to eke out another small meal from it but even that will be pathetic.

Reaching the shore, I jump into the frigid water to drag the row boat (also stolen) onto the rocky sand and up to the tree-line, gathering randomly collected branches to camouflage it on the off chance anyone else invades my sanctuary.

No one knows I'm here.

I suspect they'll think to look for me here eventually, but it's been nine days already and to my knowledge, no one has. Luckily. I'm not sure how long I'll last out here, with winter coming soon. Maybe if I'm out here long enough, in the elements and with little to nothing to eat, I'll end up begging for that jail cell that waits for me. It'll be warm, right? And dry. Hopefully, anyway. Both of those things sound pretty good right about now.

Taking my fish back to the campsite, I carefully pick my way around fallen trees and boulders. It would be just my luck to fall and break a leg out here. I'd most certainly die in a few days.

A voice inside my head—the nasty one—tells me the world would be better off if that happened. But I do what I always do: ignore it. I'm good at ignoring shit, even when that shit is me.

Everything I know now, I didn't know two weeks ago. I didn't know how to catch and gut a fish. I didn't know how to make a shelter, little more than a lean-to, really. I didn't know how to start a fire on my own. Thank Jesus for matches, but they're getting damp and besides, they're almost gone now.

I try to keep the fire low, so that it's not spotted from the mainland or from a passing ship but I figure it's just a matter of time before something gives me away. Teenagers will come out here with a case of beer and spot me skulking in the bushes or catch a whiff of smoke. It's just a matter of time.

But I've already resolved to use the time wisely. I need to figure out a way to…to what? Evade capture forever? That's what I thought I was doing at first. Maybe swim out and stowaway on a ship, let it take me to some faraway land where I can get lost among people who don't speak my language and therefore won't ask me any questions.

I was an idiot. The ships are too far out and the water is too cold. I barely made it to the island in the stolen boat. Being woefully out of shape has not helped anything I've had to do lately.

There's a lot to be said for trial and error though. And Swiss army knives. I bought mine just to have a good bottle opener on me at all times but the thing has been invaluable to me since the shit hit the fan. I've used it for everything from cutting small branches to cleaning fish to opening clam and oyster shells. If I'm out here long enough, I'll probably find other uses for it too. It also is somewhat comforting to know I have a weapon, no matter how small. I figure if I have to, I could always plunge the blade into a throat or maybe an eye. That would entail me having to be too damn close to an enemy so I hope nothing arises that would put me in a situation like that, but just in case.

I guess maybe I haven't been using the time wisely after all. Just figuring out how to not die of exposure has been a challenge and occupied all of my time. A good lesson maybe if I am to become a mountain man but I doubt that's in the cards for me.

Taking out the knife, I clean the fish I caught today on a flat rock, doing the best I can, shivering a little in the cold rain. I don't even know what kind of fish it is. That's what I get for being a city kid my whole life. We see the fish after they're cooked, if we see them at all. It's never been my favorite dish though. I've always been more of a beef and chicken kind of guy. But, I'm making due, I suppose.

Above me, lightning flashes and I pause, waiting for the thunder, counting off seconds in my head. I get to number eight but I'm not sure what it means. Is the storm eight miles out? Why did I never bother to learn shit like this in school?

Soon it will be too dark to see an inch in front of my face, so I hurry with my trusty silver blade, pulling out red, steaming guts from the fish's slit belly and tossing them away into a stand of brush and then wiping my gore-streaked hands on my already disgusting pants.

The rain begins to fall harder and I realize I was stupid to think I'd be able to build a fire today. So, do I eat the fish raw? I know people do it in some parts of the world, even in *this* part, but I don't know if I have the stomach for it. Maybe I'm not hungry enough yet. But I don't want it to go to waste either. It took me a long time to catch it and there have been a couple days when I haven't caught anything. What if tomorrow is another day like that?

I steel myself, rip a chunk of fish meat out and shove it into my mouth quickly, trying to get it down my throat while making as little contact with my tongue as possible.

Gagging, I hack it up and fight not to vomit on top of it.

Fuck.

Now I'm getting pissed. Both at myself and this whole fucking mess I'm in. It's not fair. I'm not a bad guy. I just made a really stupid mistake and now my whole life is fucked because of it.

I grab what's left of the fish and whip it into the same area I've been tossing the guts. I'm soaked down to my skin and I need to get under the pitiful thing I've been calling a shelter.

Huddling on the ground with my knees drawn up and my arms wrapped around them, I keep cursing under my breath and then realize I don't even need to be. I could scream at the top of my lungs and no one would hear me. There aren't even any animals here that I've seen with the exception of birds. And fish of course. Always with the fucking fish.

And, just like that, a flash of lightning coincides with a flash of genius.

I could just kill myself.

I mean, why not? The life that lies ahead of me will be nothing but misery anyway. Endless torture. Probably in the way of rape, if the stories are true.

Pulling my little Swiss army knife out of my pocket once more, I open it and study the blade. It's about three inches. Is that enough? I want to slice, not saw.

Thunder booms and I jump and shiver harder. Coming out here was the stupidest idea ever—the capper to a lifetime of immensely stupid ideas.

The rain is pounding now and even beneath the lean-to, I'm getting drenched. Water drips off the tip of my nose and down my cheeks, mingling with the tears I hadn't known were streaming until this precise moment.

Am I really contemplating suicide? Isn't that the ultimate cowardice? Or maybe it's the ultimate bravery.

The sea roils on the beach, slamming into the shore like Thor's hammer. I can see a portion of the beach from my camp and the water is steadily drawing closer to the tree-line. If it continues towards me, I'll have to search for higher ground. Or should I do that right now? Be proactive for the first time in my pathetic little life?

I regard the blade in my hand again. I'll still have it tomorrow.

A gust of wind pummels me with water and the lean-to goes flying. Branches sail into the air and whirl away, high into the darkened sky and out of sight.

The rain makes it hard to breathe—I'm practically choking on it as it explodes in my face, driven by the gale.

Struggling to my feet, I look northward, towards a small hill, the only higher ground I've explored so far. I was lazy. Thought I'd have plenty of time to check everything out later.

And now that I think about it, that would be a great metaphor for my entire life.

Fuck, I've been such an idiot.

I start off towards the hill, the wind whipping pieces of tree and brush at my body. The rain feels like spinning razors against my face and hands. I keep hold of the knife as I travel, the sea roaring at my back, a hungry lion gaining on its prey.

This night will be a long one and I don't know if I'm strong enough to survive it but I know for sure that I'm too weak to end my life on my own. Not yet. But maybe someday.

Maybe soon.

## CHAPTER NINE—The Junkie (5)

The third degree again.

I went back to the bar and didn't tell them about Luna. By then I was pretty jittery and just wanted to escape, as stupid as that sounds, even to myself.

The shit Luna told me is insane and I didn't much want to think about it. Still don't. So I went and took my 'medicine' and let myself fly away.

I come back from my mini vacation sweating like a pig and completely terrified. The worst I've been so far.

Halleck leans forward, sitting in the chair across from me, his eyes glinting with excitement.

-Tell me what you saw.

I do, as much as I can, but it comes out too quickly for his liking. I just want to get it out and forget about it but Halleck wants to know every detail.

-Why were you hiding on the island?

-I don't know.

-What was your crime?

-I don't know.

-How can that be? You were there. In his head. Which is *your* head.

-No it isn't. That definitely was not my fucking head.

-Of course it was. A version of you anyway. You should have been able to know everything about him as sure as you know everything about yourself. You must have known what he did—what *you* did—to be hiding like that.

-I have no fucking idea. Can I have a beer now?

-Did he sense your presence?

-I…I don't think so.

-Curious. All the others did, correct?

-I'm not sure. I guess. Maybe.

-Then he must have.

-Okay, fine. He must have. Are we done now?

Halleck is clearly losing his patience with me. Color starts to rise up from his neck, tinting his cheeks pink.

-Do you think we're fucking around here? That we're doing this for the sole purpose of getting you—a lowlife junkie—high for free? You think we're doing this because we pity you? Or even *like* you? We had a deal, Eon, and I intend to hold you to it even if I have to strap you down and keep you from ever seeing daylight again. Am I making myself clear? You are expendable.

I don't know what to say for a while. Normally if someone threatened me like that, I'd probably explode. Threats have always been the thing that piss me off the worst. I'd rather have someone lie to me than threaten me. But I bite my tongue now, not because I'm a perfectly calm Buddhist monk, but because I want to keep taking the shit. I want to get back to being the rock star. I know I can. It's just like a game of Russian roulette. You only have to pull the trigger so many times before you hit pay dirt.

As soon as the thought is complete, I realize what an awful analogy it is. Maybe I should compare it instead to playing the lottery, back when there was a lottery to play. But the odds were so stacked against everyone, it's not a particularly cheery analogy either.

-When do I get back to being the rock star?

Halleck gives me a look that says he thinks I'm the absolute biggest idiot he has ever had the misfortune of encountering. But then, bafflingly, he smiles.

-It could be the next time. You never know.

I'm skeptical and I guess my face shows it.

-But probably not, right?

He holds up his hands in a *who knows* gesture.

-The universe is a vast and immense thing. It could very well be infinite, as the scientists of old have always speculated. Or it could be finite. You could just have to cycle through half a dozen alternate realities before you start back at the beginning again. Or, you might not ever see that particular lifetime again, even if you take the drug every day for a hundred years.

I must look distressed at this answer, because he goes on, smiling wider.

-I myself believe the chances are good that you'll return—sooner than later—to the life you seem to be so smitten with, though I have no idea why you are so captivated by it. Did that person seem exceptionally happy to you?

I take a second to think about the question. It's a good one.

-Well, he seemed exceptionally rich. And admired.

Halleck sits back in his chair and steeples his fingers.

-And that's all you care about? Wealth? Admiration?

-Well...I'm sure it doesn't hurt.

He nodded.

-True. True. But have you thought about what it might mean if together you and I somehow figure out how to make this drug more precise? If we can understand how to get you exactly where you want to be? *Every* time? Have you considered that at all, Eon?

I hadn't. Was that the goal here? Had it always been the goal? Because it would have been nice if I'd been told that.

-You.

Halleck points at me with one of his long, spider-leg

fingers.

-*You* are the key, Eon. Which is what I'm trying to tell you. Why I need you to recall every moment of your journeys. Every detail and emotion. Every facet of your thoughts, feelings, memories. With every tidbit you share, the closer we get to cracking the mystery. Don't you see?

He sounds like he's talking gibberish but I nod just the same. In truth, I'm thinking about Luna. She told me how dangerous this drug was. Not for my body necessarily but for other people. For the minds I inhabit, is how she put it. I don't really understand most of what she said, any more than I understand what Halleck is saying. I've never been a science guy. Hell, I'm barely an English guy. And not only that, but I'm just not sure how I can possibly be affecting anyone when I'm on one of my trips. It's just a fucking trip. When you take acid and hallucinate the moon blowing up, once you come down, you see the moon is still perfectly intact. No harm, no foul.

I get this isn't exactly the same, but I think it's close enough. Yeah, the guy with the telescope and the family seemed freaked out but was it even real? Does he remember it? Is *he* real? I'm starting to think maybe this whole thing, including both Halleck and Luna, is a load of horseshit. Yeah, *they* obviously believe this supernatural shit is going down, but is it really?

-Eon! Are you even in town?

-What? Oh, yeah. Sorry. Spaced out for a minute.

The basement door opens and a second later Hoop is pounding down the stairs in his heavy steel-toed boots. When he reaches the bottom, he gives Halleck a meaningful look I can't decipher. Halleck looks back at me.

-Excuse us, Eon. I'll be back shortly. In the meantime, please think back on what you learned during your most recent journey. Anything you can glean could be helpful.

-Right.

The two of them plod up the stairs and I hear the door close.

This is really beginning to suck. They clearly don't trust me, but I suppose that's okay because I sure as shit don't trust them.

I get up from my seat and start pacing around the cement floor of the basement. A few areas are covered with cheap knock-off oriental rugs, which seems somewhat strange to me but whatever. I have to be careful not to trip on the lips of the rugs though.

A tapping makes me look up and to the right. Luna is peering into one of the basement windows, blonde hair falling over one eye.

*What the fuck is she doing here?*

I walk over to the window and look up at it, holding out my hands to say, *what the fuck are you doing here?*

She points to her wrist, on which there is no watch, then holds up her hand, all five fingers splayed.

Five minutes.

She wants me to meet her in five minutes?

I crinkle my brow and shake my head, jerking a thumb over my shoulder at the stairs, hoping she'll get what I'm trying to convey.

In reply, she shakes her head back at me, flashing her outward facing palm again.

I don't know what to do. I'd *like* to go talk to her-I mean, you never know when you might get lucky, right? And she's pretty hot, always in her leather, whether she's crazy as a shithouse rat or not. But I doubt Halleck is finished with me. Of course, he did just get pulled away too. Maybe for something more important than interrogating me until I bleed from my eyeballs from boredom?

Hanging out with Luna has to be better than that, doesn't it?

Halleck can wait, I decide. Anything I can tell him now, I can tell him just as good later.

I give Luna the thumbs up sign, hoping she'll smile, but she doesn't. Just nods grimly and disappears from sight.

The cellar door opens again and here come the gruesome twosome, hurrying down the stairs. Halleck starts talking before he even reaches the bottom.

-We're going to dose you again, Eon.

-What? Now? But—

-Yes, now.

-I was hoping for a little r and r, you know? Just a little time off. Maybe get something to eat.

-You can eat after. Sit down.

Hoop is already prepping the syringe in his hands as Halleck marches over to me.

-Sit down.

My stomach does a little cartwheel thing. I'm suddenly very nervous.

-What's going on?

Halleck roars at me.

*-Sit down or so help me god, I will leave you in a gutter like a fucking rat!*

Again with the threats.

-Fuck you.

I start to push by him and he steps back just far enough to land a punch to my jaw that knocks me off balance and sends me crashing to the floor.

While I'm still stunned and reeling, Hoop approaches and together they get the job done.

## CHAPTER TEN—The Rider

The car is falling fast but I keep the gun aimed at her as she sits beside me, gripping the safety bar in both hands. Down one slope we go, my stomach clenched. I've never cared for heights and have never been brave enough to ride a rollercoaster before, but I'm sure as hell riding one now.

She and I are the only ones riding it in fact, racing through the night sky, first up, then down and back up again. Spinning around hairpin curves so fast and hard that I'm positive I will not survive this. I will go flying out of this rickety little car on the rickety old tracks and whirl end over end, landing on the concrete almost two hundred feet below with a wet smack I will thankfully not hear. Probably won't even feel.

Below us, red and blue lights flash, coming into focus…going out of focus. I'm brave enough to look down once and see the crowd of officers gathered down there, their faces tiny pink and brown blurred specks, and I never look down again. It makes me too queasy.

The guy who runs the rollercoaster was more than cooperative. I showed him my gun, told him to get everyone else off the coaster and let us on. Keep it going no matter what. If not, the pretty lady was going to end up without a head.

The guy, sporting faded tattoos and a grayed handlebar mustache, didn't seem all that alarmed at the sight of the gun. Maybe he's seen a lot of them in his day. He told me in his gravelly voice to keep cool and did as he was told. People filed off the coaster, none the wiser, but complaining their ride had been too short.

The other people who'd been waiting with us—of course we waited our turn like everyone else—grumbled loudest of all and I was tempted to show *them* the gun too, but I didn't. I told Mr. Mustache to not call the cops and everything would be fine and he agreed, but obviously he's not a man of his word because about five minutes later, a slew of cruisers showed up, sirens screeching, bubbles whirling.

I can't think about any of that now though. I have to concentrate on the task at hand, assuming I can manage not to puke or shit my damn pants.

-Are you sure this is the only way?

She nods frantically, her hair blowing back, whipping wildly.

-This is the only thing I could think of.

She's shouting to be heard, gasping. I know the feeling. It's hard to get the words out when you're getting punched in the face by a hundred mile an hour winds.

The motion, she'd said, would save her life somehow but we had to get there soon and we can't stop. The motion—the coaster—has to keep going until she figures out what to do next. Making her my 'hostage' was her idea. She thought it would be the only way to get her on and make them not stop the coaster. But now we're here, I'm kind of wishing she'd just brought the gun herself and threatened suicide.

Just the thought makes me feel guilty though. How selfish can I be? We're in this together. And besides, the suicide threat probably wouldn't have worked anyway. The cops would have just showed up with a shrink to talk to her and stopped the coaster immediately.

We plummet down another drop and I squeeze my eyes closed. There's a very good chance I'm not going to survive this night and, unless she figures out a way to keep her own life from ending before we stop, she'll not live to see tomorrow either.

We're both fucked.

Either this goddamn amusement park ride will give me a heart attack, or the cops will shoot me dead.

The fact is driven home even further when we notice a police chopper suddenly on the scene, buzzing above us like a prehistoric mosquito, its spotlight trying to keep up with the speeding car.

I don't get a very good look at it but it occurs to me that they might try to shoot me from up there. It seems unlikely, given the speed of the coaster and the fact I can't imagine anyone being a good enough sharp-shooter that they would risk missing me and hitting her, but once the thought is in my head, I can't shake it. My skull is going to shatter and that will be the end of it.

-They might try to shoot me!

She looks terrified but she's looked terrified since this whole thing began a couple hours ago when she first received the instructions on how to save her life. She didn't go into a lot of explanation regarding that part. I only know she hasn't been feeling well. Migraines have left her shaking and sobbing for the last day and then, not long ago, she began rocking back and forth on the bed, going faster and faster until I was sure she was having a mental breakdown.

She explained that it eased the pain a little and even a little was better than no relief at all.

But then, she insisted I take her on a drive. I almost brought her right to the hospital but she begged me not to, demanding instead that I drive faster and faster until I was sure we were going to go right off the road.

I drove up to the hills above the city, where there's

usually less traffic on the curvier roads. Once there, she sighed audibly, saying the headache had eased even more. The faster I took the curves and the hills, the less pain she was in. That went on for about half an hour and the next thing I knew, she was ordering me to take her to the coaster and handing me the pistol I keep in the glove box.

-We're slowing down.

Opening my eyes, I see she's right.

So this is it. The end is approaching and I'm petrified but also the tiniest bit relieved. The cops will get her to a hospital finally. See what's happening in her head. Remove the tumor if that's what it is. Hopefully, I'll be kept informed of the situation from my jail cell, assuming I make it to one without being riddled with bullet holes. Maybe the doctors, once they figure out what's wrong with her and see I had no choice, will testify on my behalf and I won't have to serve as much time.

I cling to this hope mightily.

Beside me, she starts to scream, letting go of the safety bar and clasping her hands to her head. Blood begins to ooze from her nose, smearing back along her cheeks when we hit another drop.

My screams join hers, but I'm screaming words.

-Keep it going! Stop slowing it down!

I doubt anyone can hear me and the tattooed man has been pulled away from the scene, as have all the other innocent bystanders. We probably have the entire amusement part to ourselves and under other circumstances that would be exceptionally romantic. Ridiculously, I remember hearing on the local news about a couple who'd gotten married on this very coaster last summer. I wonder if we're riding in the same car as they did. What are the chances?

Our train of cars slows even further and I know soon

we won't be going fast enough to make it up the next incline. They're stopping the coaster. What else can they do? They have to take the chance that I won't really shoot her, hope they can talk me out of it, get her to safety. It's their only choice. They can't let us ride the rollercoaster forever.

*-There has to be another way!*

She ignores me and keeps shrieking, blood now trickling from the corners of her eyes. She's dying. I doubt she even knows where she is anymore.

Slower, slower.

Slowest and then stop at the platform where we first got on. Half a dozen cops are waiting, weapons drawn, shouting at me, their faces pallid at the sight of her, slumped forward and bloody, barely conscious.

They think I did this to her.

*-Drop your fucking weapon!*

*-Drop it, asshole! Drop it NOW!*

*-Toss it!*

Too many commands at one time. I let the gun fall from my hand and clatter to the bottom of the car.

*-You have to help her! She's dying!*

I'm a sobbing wreck, reaching out for her until I'm ordered to raise my hands and that's when it happens. A combination of a crack and a pop and my wife's head is gone. Just exploded into a red, white and gray mess that hits me full-force in the face.

I scream through the gore and cops are yelling, cursing, backing up. I hear the word 'bomb' multiple times and think, *no shit, Sherlock.* The thought is inexplicably hilarious and I stop my screaming and crying to laugh instead. A crazy, high-pitched laugh I've never heard before. It sounds like the laugh of the truly insane and forever damned but I can't help it. I know it's wrong, not the reaction I should be having to such a horrific, nightmarish event, but it just goes on and on and on.

I'm grabbed roughly and dragged out of the coaster car, thrown face down on the concrete platform and handcuffed. I fully expect police brutality, but no one hits or kicks me. Maybe they're too shocked.

When they lift me up a little while later, one cop gets in my face, shouting questions I have no answers for.

My wife is dead and now we might never know why. I taste her blood on my lips and my chest heaves. It could be laughing or crying. Right now both are pretty much the same thing.

## CHAPTER ELEVEN—The Junkie (6)

The first thing I do is scream, not because I'm tied up but because there's blood and brains all over my face.

Or so I think for a terrifying instant.

I come out of it and this time—it takes me mere seconds to discover—I *am* strapped down. Still in the basement, but not in the usual chair. Instead, Halleck or Hoop have kindly gifted me a comfy cot to stretch out on and be shackled to with thick leather straps.

-What the fuck!

Lifting my head, I look around and see Harvey at long last. He's seated in my old chair and it's on my lips to say something to him, but then I notice his face doesn't look quite right. Warped somehow. Like the left side of his face is bulging oddly and I flash on the time I had an abscessed tooth and my face looked kind of like that until my pal Bruce yanked the tooth out with pliers. I was high as a fucking kite and barely conscious when he did it so it wasn't a big deal at the time. The big deal came hours later when my high wore off and I was still bleeding buckets out of my mouth and had to talk Bruce into stitching up the hole with sewing thread. There were shards of tooth imbedded in my gums for years after. They're still there to this very day, in fact.

Studying Harvey now though, seeing his gray pallor, and a dribble of dried blood on his right temple, I put two and two together to come up with he is seriously fucking *dead*.

Shot in the head by the looks of it and someone is going to get an earful when they get back down here to dose me or torture me or whatever it is they plan on doing to me next. I definitely don't appreciate being tied up but being left alone with a corpse seems particularly cruel to me. Especially since I know the guy. Or *knew* him, I suppose.

I test the restraints and find they're pretty solid. Kudos to whichever fuck did this to me. My only recourse is to start yelling my fucking head off so that's what I do, shouting for help until my throat is hoarse. There must be someone in the bar upstairs, right? Sooner or later, someone is bound to ask who the hell is doing all the screaming. Even shit-faced, I'm pretty sure I'd be able to tell that not everything is copasetic if I heard a dude yelling his damn balls off for help.

I can feel the muscles in my neck, arms and legs bunching up and bulging as I struggle to get free and shout at the same time. Sweat is beading up all over my body, which is pissing me off even more. I fucking hate to sweat. It's too close to work.

All my struggles pay off though because a couple minutes later I hear the door open and sure enough, here comes Hoop looking like he's ready to commit a homicide. Well, *another* homicide.

He growls at me in a way I've never heard before.

-Shut the fuck up, Eon! You want to end up like your buddy there?

Again with the threats.

-*Untie me, you sick fuck! Right fucking now!*

I try to sound as ferocious as he does, but I doubt I succeed. I'm just not a tough guy, as the pain in my jaw where Halleck hit me keeps reminding me.

Hoop stands over my prone body and points a meaty finger in my face.

-I'm not fucking around with you anymore, Eon. This

is seriously deep shit we're in.

-What do you mean, 'we'? I didn't do shit except apparently get fucking kidnapped by you rat shit eating fuckers!

-Believe it or not, this is for your own fucking good.

-Oh, really? Was putting a bullet in Harvey's head for *his* own good?

-That couldn't be helped.

Am I mistaken or does Hoop look like he might be feeling a little guilty about that particular incident? I think so, so I press it.

-What a scumbag, shit-heel move, man. Harvey was a good guy. I think he had kids somewhere. Fucking dickhead.

-Halleck killed him, genius. He was getting too mouthy, telling people what he knew. He told one guy about Sennacherib's! Came asking about Satellite, where could he get the shit. I had to play fucking dumb. Once Halleck heard about it...

Hoop sticks out an index finger and drags it across the front of this own throat.

-He's not fucking messing around, man.

This gives me serious cause for concern and I start hollering again.

-Un-fucking-tie me, you prick! He'll kill me too!

What was once Hoop's pretend knife turns into a real fist, which he brandishes over me.

 -I'm serious, man. I'll knock you out.

Then he pauses, as if making sense of what I just said.

-Who did you tell?

-I...huh?

-Why would Halleck kill you too, unless you told someone?

I have to think fast, which has never been my forte.

-No one! I just assume—you know, silly fucking me—that being tied up means I'm dead fucking meat here. Let me go before he gets back.

Hoop looks suspiciously down at me and I do my best to appear innocent.

-Come on! This is no joke!

-You think you're telling me that? This is my fucking bar! My living! And now look at this shit! I have one guy dead in my basement and another one tied the fuck up. I could end up doing serious time for this shit.

Starting to pace, Hoop rubs both hands over his bald head. I feel a little better, hoping the idea of hitting me has left his brain in favor of shitting his pants instead.

-That's my point, Hoop. You want *two* dead guys in your basement? Let me go before he gets back. I won't say shit. Hell, I'll fucking get out of Dodge. There's nothing here for me anyway.

The upstairs door opens again and both of us go pale, looking towards the stairs with dread. We yelp when the body of a man comes tumbling down the stairs, yipping in pain. I fully expect Halleck to come down, following in the body's wake and I have to strain my neck, lifting my head in order to see that Halleck isn't chasing after the fallen body because the fallen body is his.

Hoop backs up several steps and I hear him make a high-pitched whining noise, like a scared dog.

I'm still struggling to see what's going on, simultaneously trying to free myself from the restraints. I see boots coming down the stairs and I'm confused by the sight of them, but then come the legs and I'm even more confused.

When she's all the way down, Luna kicks Halleck in the face, hard. Blood and teeth fly and he makes a low, groaning sound that might be one of the most pitiful things I've ever heard.

-Luna!

Hoop looks at me, amazed.

-You know this bitch?

I don't know if it was her intention all along or if it was being called a nasty word, but Luna walks over to Hoop and punches him square in the face.

He's a stocky guy and doesn't go down, but he definitely wobbles, stumbling backwards as blood gushes from his mouth. He reels back, swinging up a fist from his hip but Luna kicks it away and lays into him again. I have time to wonder if she's secretly a ninja. Everything is happening in slow motion. Hoop is down—maybe unconscious—and Luna is at my side, undoing the bounds at my wrists and ankles.

I try to smile.

-Sorry I didn't meet you in five.

-Let me guess. You were tied up?

-Good guess.

Once I'm free and on my feet, we both step over Hoop and start for the stairs. I look one last time at Harvey, then look away. There goes my best connection.

We have to step over Halleck too, then we're up and out, through the bar and into what I'm surprised to see is still night.

A long black car is waiting at the curb for us and Luna practically shoves me into the backseat, climbing in after me, the car screeching off before she's even got the door closed.

In the driver's seat is a man, turned around to examine me, eyeing me with doubt.

-This is him?

-Yep.

Luna turns in her own seat, looking out the rear

window.

I give the dude the same look he's giving me.

-Who are you?

Answering for him, Luna faces front again.

-His name is Circe.

The guy gives the tiniest of nods.

-Pleasure.

I nod back, alternately rubbing each of my sore wrists.

-Cool name.

The guy raises an eyebrow.

-Thanks, *Eon*.

I frown.

-That's my last name, man.

-Sure it is.

Luna leans forward and I hope she's gonna pound Circe in the face but she doesn't.

-We have to get him inside fast. He's going to spin again soon.

Circe faces front, gives me the stink-eye from the rearview.

-How soon?

-Maybe five minutes, tops.

-Fuck.

Circe groans and stomps harder on the gas, causing both Luna and I to press back into our seats.

I touch Luna's leg.

-Spin?

-You're riding again, friend. You passed the point of no return the last time you spun.

-And...that's bad, huh?

She gives me a look and I shrug.

-Well, *I* don't know. I have no idea what you're talking about.

-We have to get you to Atropos.

-Where's that?
-It's not a place, it's a person.
-Oh, okay. Well, then who's that?
I don't stick around long enough to hear her answer.

## CHAPTER TWELVE—The Survivor

Picking through the rubble is an almost meditative pastime at this point. I try to keep my eyes and ears open for other scavengers but I'm so damn tired and weak all the time that I've been snuck up on before. Not good. Knocked out, stripped, robbed of everything, violated. They would have eaten me too if I hadn't had a few cans of food when they caught me. They were so giddy, I was forgotten almost as soon as they were finished with me. Left naked and bleeding.

They were savage children, grown up in this harsh environment. Thievery, rape and killing were all they knew-a means to an end—the end being they were the living, unscathed for the moment and their bellies weren't scraping rock bottom.

Not all of the city has been leveled, but I've found that this ruined area is, surprisingly, the safest. Where buildings still stand, wars are fought, sometimes with stones and pipes, sometimes with automatic weapons, but the ammo won't last forever, while the stones just might. They'll outlast us anyway.

I spend the most time in the destroyed parts of cities, bedding down with rats and sometimes eating the same scraps they do. I've found following them, studying them, will often lead to what amounts to riches these days. Once, on a particularly blessed day, they led me to a buried bag of dry dog food. Fifteen pounds worth, barely touched by the vermin. I ate like a king for nearly two weeks, dragging the thing into the backseat of a car beneath a collapsed parking garage. The accommodations were tight and more than a little claustrophobic but it was worth it. A good hiding place and grub. I only went out to collect rain water in a few empty tin cans and I did that in the dead of night, my usual scrounging hours.

Here though, on the south side, most everything has been picked clean. People passing through, moving on to warmer climes, just like me. That was the plan anyway but now I'm starting to think I might just be better off where I am. I try to go wherever people aren't. People are dangerous. People have always been dangerous but now there's no pretending about it. No hiding from it.

I just keep moving on my own, no ties. Those are long gone.

Limping past a shattered mall, I need to find somewhere to bed down soon. My left knee feels like it's going to explode and it won't support my weight much longer. Smashed it about two years ago in a fall and it's never been the same since. Hurts the worst on rainy days though and the overcast sky is already spitting down on me, getting ready to open up and unleash hell.

There's an apartment complex a little ways up from the mall and even though I'm scared shitless some roamers might be holed up there already, that's where I'm headed, hoping for a dry spot anywhere. Safe and dry until daylight doesn't seem like a whole lot to ask for but it's close to everything nowadays. If the spot I find feels safe enough, I'll sleep on through the day, rest the knee and search for food tomorrow night.

I stick to the shadows, taking my time, watching where I step so I don't inadvertently kick something that might make a racket and draw attention to me.

Everything is dark and tomb silent. Even the scavenging animals have moved on from this place.

Studying the windows from a safe distance, I see no

flicker of flames, no blur of light from a shielded flashlight. Nothing is moving.

I wait, huddled by a big oak that's miraculously still alive, though all its leaves have fallen and blown away a couple weeks ago now. More than half an hour passes by my count and stillness abides.

Gathering up my courage, I move cautiously towards the buildings, aiming for one not too close to the street, but not too far away either.

The parking lot is nearly empty but a few stray cars are still parked here and there, rusting hulks with smashed windows, their doors hanging open, their seats gone.

There are both first and second floor apartments in this complex and second is almost always safer, so I choose one at random, climbing the stairs as quickly as my bad leg will allow.

The door is only hanging from one hinge but at least it exists, which is more fortunate than some of the other apartments. Hell, a lot of the places don't exist at all anymore, either being fully or partially collapsed or, in some cases, destroyed by fire.

But the one I've chosen is relatively intact and for that reason I expect it to be already occupied. I slip out the bat I carry—it sticks out of my backpack for easy access—and hold it at the ready as I slowly push open the broken door and ease myself over the threshold.

If there are people in here, I hope with all my might they're sleeping and I can slip out again, with them never the wiser.

It's pitch-black inside and it takes a minute for my eyes to adjust. When they finally do, I waste no time, moving through the small apartment like a crippled soldier, examining the bedroom, bathroom, kitchen and living room in less than two minutes. I also explore the closets.

Nothing, though I do find evidence that someone, or maybe several someones, has camped out here before. There are blankets on the floor in the kitchen, which is smart because it's in the center of the place, away from any windows.

I decide it's where I'll spend the rest of the night as well. What little of it there is left.

It's regrettable that I have to stop at all during the hours of darkness, but my damn knee is insisting on it, as it does more and more lately.

No matter.

We do what we must.

I use a mini-flashlight to kick around the stained and stinking blankets already here, ensure there's nothing nesting in them, and take off my pack, place it nearby and slowly lower myself to the floor, leaning my back against the mostly cracked and crooked cabinets.

Sighing, I realize just how exhausted I am. Only twenty-eight but my body, I think, is that of a seventy year old. And not a particularly spry one.

I pray to a god I don't believe in that I make it through the rest of the night and tomorrow. Please let me rest here, undisturbed and protected from any roamers that may happen by.

It takes me a bit to be brave enough to close my eyes, but I eventually do, though my ears are still alert for as long as I can manage it.

I think about the old days, so long ago, before war and disease ravaged our world and turned it into what it is today: rubble crawling with savages desperate to get you before you get them. There aren't many of us left who remember what it used to be like before skylines fell and suburbs burned.

Something prickles the back of my neck and my eyes

open. Looking around, I see nothing has changed and only silence looms large.

But still, there's the feeling of being watched. Or…

Growing nervous, I place my right hand on the bat lying beside me. My eyes tick around the kitchen, studying everything I can see with renewed interest, though in the dark there's not much to see except shadows. I raise my left hand and examine it as though I've never seen it before. Why does it seem so old? So many scars? It clearly hasn't been washed in days. Maybe weeks.

I lift my arm higher and take a whiff of my own armpit, grimacing at the stench before dropping it again. I look down at what I'm wearing, little more than rags, and I'm overcome with fright but also an intense curiosity.

My heart begins hammering in my chest. What's going on here? Am I finally losing my mind? I feel like an alien in my own body.

But, no. That's not quite right. It's more like I'm *sharing* my mind with a stranger…a latent being.

I swallow what feels like a lemon lodged in my throat and then something even stranger happens. A sense of peace washes over me. My racing heart begins to slow down, my breathing, which had also begun to quicken, returns to normal.

Closing my eyes once more, I feel relaxed in a way that hasn't happened since I don't remember when. Certainly since before the civil wars.

It's an epiphany, I realize. There is something inside me that's been there all along. I was just too preoccupied to listen.

It's God after all.

We are, all of us, not alone.

There are many hardships, yes, but the voice in my head is not mine and, as it is not threatening, it can't be anything but a supreme being. In fact, it's not even so much a voice as it is a...comforting layer of pure inner light.

I wish the churches hadn't been the first structures to burn. It would be nice to go inside one, sit in a pew and marvel at the wonder of the universe and the one who created it all with love and gentle kindness. But, if I can't find a church, I will make one myself, somehow.

I will find a way. I'll show everyone the light burning in my chest and point out it's in theirs as well. Everyone can find it—all they need is a moment to reflect and the peace and a safe space to do it in.

Thank You so much for Your compassion and devotion, for the eternal, undying love. I will give it back in kind and it will never be forgotten again.

I'm vaguely aware of a rumbling sound and at first assume it's my stomach. When was the last time I ate? Then my body is jarred and I come fully awake, still in the backseat of the car, though it takes me a couple seconds to get my bearings.

-He's back.

Turning my head, I see Luna leaning over her half of the back seat and into mine, peering into my face.

I blink and begin to tremble slightly. The trip—did these people call it a *spin* before?—comes back to me and I'm immediately frightened.

The guy in the front seat turns around to gaze at me. It takes me a long moment to place his name.

Oh, yeah. Circe.

-Nice to see you again, Eon.

I grunt at him and attempt to sit up straighter while turning to Luna.

-What the fuck was that? I didn't even get dosed.

After thinking about this for a moment, I wonder if it's true.

-Did I?

She shook her head.

-You don't need to be dosed anymore. Almost without fail, six times seems to be the charm.

-The charm?

Ignoring the question, she continues.

-From now on, you'll be spinning with no help from any drug.

-But...*how?*

-The drug repeatedly sparked synapses in your brain, creating a pathway that's not normally lit. Think of the drug as a flint stone against straw. It sparks repeatedly, but then, with enough strikes, the straw will burst into flame. Understand?

I stare blankly for a moment.

-If that's true, what happens to the straw, which I assume in this analogy is my brain? It'll burn up, right?

The driver, Circe, is the one who replies.

-Pretty much, yeah.

Luna gives him a chilly glance before returning her attention to me.

-For some spinners, yes. But not all. Some take a very long time to burn out.

I really don't like the sound of that.

-Burn out?

She clears her throat.

-We'll talk about it later. There's plenty of time, and besides, we've arrived.

Looking out the front of the car, I see we've pulled into a long, curving driveway bordered by thick trees on either side.

-We've arrived where, exactly?

-Atropos calls this place Olympia, which was a sacred place to the ancient Greeks.

This explanation tells me nothing but as we round the next and final curve, I see an extremely tall, extremely ornate wrought iron gate attached to equally tall stone pillars which are, in turn, attached to a huge stone wall surrounding what I assume to be acres of property.

Beyond the gate, after another hundred yards of circular driveway, there's a mansion, the likes of which I have never seen in real life.

My jaw drops, not only at the sight of the gigantic

property, but also at the two armed guards at the gate. They're also gigantic, each wielding what appear to be AK-47's and bandoliers of extra ammo.

-Holy fucking Christ.

Circe smirks.

-Just about.

One of the guards, a guy with a face like a bulldog, opens the gate manually and Circe drives us through, past a dead water fountain and up to the house.

I keep thinking about how this can't be real. I'm having another trip—or spin, as my companions call it— if *they're* even real. I feel like I have to question everything now and it's not a good feeling.

Once we're all out of the car, we walk the gravel drive up to the house and encounter two more armed guards, nearly identical to the first two. They make me nervous. I wonder if they're cops or what.

Luna touches my arm as we approach the front door.

-Relax. It'll be fine.

Circe gives an amused snort and I'm forced to wonder just what the fuck his problem is.

The guards let us by without a word. A quick nod from Luna is all it takes to gain access to this mansion apparently.

Magically, the oak door swings open without so much as a knock, and sure enough, it's another guy with a gun. I'm a little disappointed. I was hoping Alfred Pennyworth would be the one greeting us.

We enter into a wide foyer, stepping onto what I think is a real marble floor, a vast staircase directly in front of us.

Descending the staircase is a girl dressed all in white, maybe seventeen or so, blonde dreadlocks standing out in sharp contrast to her coffee-no-cream skin. Even from a distance of fifty feet, she has the palest blue eyes I've ever seen in my entire life.

Her expression is blank and, despite this, when her gaze lands on me, I feel utterly intimidated.

As she reaches the bottom of the stairs, Luna steps forward.

-This is the man.

The girl regards Luna with mild indifference.

-I see.

Once more, her eyes find mine and it takes everything I have not to shrink back, so powerful is her presence.

She holds out a hand for shaking.

-Welcome, Mr. Eon. I am Atropos.

I take her hand, feeling more shy than I ever have before.

-Hi. Thank you.

Holding her gaze is impossible and I want to kick myself. She's little more than a child. Why am I so intimidated by her?

-I trust your journey was uneventful?

She shifts her attention to Luna.

-Nothing I couldn't handle. Though I should mention he spun in the car.

Atropos nods.

-That's unfortunate. How much time before he goes again?

-The times are getting shorter, so…another two hours, at most.

I balk at this new information.

-*Two hours! How is this even possible? What's going on?*

Atropos is unfazed by my outburst.

-We need you to be calm, Mr. Eon. Circe will show you to your room and I'll be along shortly for a discussion. I'll try to answer all your questions then.

She gives myself and the others another nod and walks off past the stairs and towards two closed doors large enough for giants to fit through.

A guard opens the doors for her and closes them behind her.

Circe whacks my arm with his fist.

-Need to change your panties, Princess?

-What the fuck?

-Come on.

He begins climbing the grand staircase and after a look from Luna, I reluctantly follow.

We pass room after room as we walk a seemingly endless hallway decorated with oil portraits of unknown women though the ages. Wall sconces burn golden and I feel like I've been teleported back to colonial times.

Circe finally stops at a door and gestures.

-This is you.

-What am I supposed to do in here?

-Nothing. Wait for Atropos to come talk to you.

With that, he walks off, going back the way we'd just come.

I want to argue, but the truth is I'm just not feeling quite up to it. I'm exhausted and shaken up by my last trip. Or spin. Whatever.

Opening the door, I enter a room which could easily have fit four of my rooms back home within it.

There's a four-poster bed, king size by the look of it, a large mahogany chest of drawers, a small writing desk in the corner, a crushed red velvet loveseat that matches both the bedspread and the curtains and two bedside tables, each with what appear to be matching Tiffany lamps on top of them.

On the opposite side of the room, across from the bed, is a small stone fireplace with an ornate maple mantel, an old-fashioned oil burning lamp atop it.

In other words, the nicest fucking digs I've ever seen in my whole life.

If this is where I get to stay, hell, I'll happily spin my life away.

Crossing the room to the window, I look out on a vast expanse of green lawn bordered by deepest forest. More of a field than a lawn really.

I'm thinking about how we could play a pretty awesome game of baseball out there when there's a gentle rap on the door.

Surprised, my voice squeaks as I turn away from the window.

-Uh…come in?

Atropos enters, arriving much sooner than I had anticipated. She closes the door behind her, but not before I get a glimpse of a guard out there. This teenager must be very important indeed.

-I trust the accommodations are to your liking?

I can feel color darkening my cheeks and I clear my throat awkwardly.

-Yeah, uh…it's a nice place you have here.

It takes all the willpower in my being not to punch myself in the face. How fucking lame can a person be?

Atropos doesn't waste any time getting to the nitty-gritty, folding her hands in front of her.

-Do you understand what's happening to you, Mr. Eon?

-Umm…not really. I mean, Luna told me a little about how I…uh…don't need Satellite to…umm…spin anymore. It will just happen whenever now, right?

She raises her chin slightly and narrows those pale, almost-white eyes.

-Do you have any questions for me?

I shift my weight uncomfortably.

-About…?

-About your spins. I imagine you've already noticed you can sense yourself sometimes.

-Excuse me?

-When you hi-jack yourself in other dimensions. The alternate Mr. Eon senses your presence, yes? But not always.

I stare at her, baffled.

-How did you…how did you know that?

She ignores the question.

-The reason for that is…

Eyeing me briefly, she seems to come to some conclusion about me. Probably my intelligence level, if I had to guess.

-Think of alternate dimensions as towns or cities. Some are miles apart. Others are side by side. When you spin into a dimension close to our own, the more likely it is that the alternate you will sense something is amiss.

-Like a glitch in the matrix?

I laugh at my own joke, but her face doesn't change. It occurs to me that she might be too young to have ever seen the sci-fi classic.

She takes a step towards me, tilting her head slightly.

-How are you feeling Mr. Eon?

Puzzled, I nervously scratch my head.

-Fine. A little tired maybe. Why do you—

## CHAPTER FOURTEEN—The Slacker

Shit work for shit pay. Story of my life. But now it's even worse. Mopping the floor in 'the dining area' of an ancient Scrummy Burger in a bright green paper hat with a matching vest and that's it—I have reached the lowest of the low.

-Excuse me!

An overweight woman is snapping her fingers to get my attention.

-I'd like some ketchup!

I try to pretend I don't hear her and keep mopping but her voice is so shrill I have to look up after only a few seconds of averting my gaze. When she makes her demand this time I point at one of the little counters near the front on the restaurant.

-Ketchup is over there.

She gives me a look like I just slapped her baby and tried to feed it a steaming spoonful of shit fresh out of my ass.

I go back to mopping and ignoring her.

It doesn't take long before John, the manager, comes out and asks to have a word with me in the back.

Sighing, I put the mop in the bucket and follow him off the floor and into a breakroom the size of a broom closet, where he reams me out for being 'rude to a customer.'

John is about twenty years old. Could almost be my son. Or at least my much younger brother.

-I'm not a fucking waiter. This isn't Elaine's.

His pimpled face turns sour. Well, *more* sour.

-I already told you not to use that language in here. And it doesn't matter if you're not a waiter. They ask for something, you get it. End of story. Understood?

I rub the bristles on my cheek and remember I didn't shave that morning. I'm surprised John hasn't mentioned it.

-And what did I tell you about coming in looking like a bum? Don't you own a razor?

Damn.

-Maybe if I wasn't making minimum wage, I could afford a goddamn razor.

John flushes bright pink, which I have to admit, gives me a certain amount of satisfaction. He'll probably go home and take his anger out on his teddy bear.

-This is your last warning.

His voice has venom in it but I can't say his threats cause me much concern.

-Okay, then. Are we done here?

-We're done.

I get out of the break room fast and leave him sitting there at the shitty Formica-topped table, glaring after me.

Back with my mop, I have to keep from groaning aloud at all the people in Scrummy Burger today. There's a parade going on outside and as a result, we're swamped and there's barely enough room to walk around, never mind mop. It's one of those days I almost wish I was working the counter or making the fries or something. But, too bad for me, I tried that once and it didn't work out so well. Accidentally gave a customer a root beer when he wanted an orange soda and apparently that was the most devastating thing that's ever happened to him.

That incident signified my first 'private meeting' with John, all of two weeks ago.

I'm stunned I've lasted as long as I have. I also

shocked I haven't gotten into a fistfight yet, the key word being '*yet*.'

Working with the public always drives home the knowledge—the indisputable *fact*—that the human race is nothing more than hate-filled, selfish cock-gobblers and if you weren't a misanthrope before the job, you'll certainly be one after the first full day of working. You'll never feel so blessed as when you clock out after your shift.

The end of the day is the only thing I think about, which is both bad and good at the same time. Good because it cheers me up somewhat but bad because I keep checking the damn clock, thinking an hour has passed and finding out it's only been ten minutes.

I can't keep up with the dining room floor anymore; people keep throwing wrappers down and crushing French fries into the tile, so fuck it. Besides, it's hard moving around and the place is so loud it sounds like a packed stadium. Not only do most people love to shove chemicals down their gullets at the rate of five-thousand calories a meal, but they also love the sounds of their own voices. Especially when they've found something to be pseudo pissed about. Which everyone in the crowd seems to be.

From the snatches of conversation I hear, it has something to do with the parade. A pride parade and there's lots of folks wearing rainbow colors and beads and whatnot, but there's lots of other people wearing crucifixes and t-shirts with bible quotes on them.

Here we go, I think, happy to be pushing my mop bucket to the back room. Sadly though, I can't hide there forever. I know this from experience. Instead, I head to the men's room, get in a stall and just hang out for a few, reading the new graffiti I'll undoubtedly be cleaning off later.

Even the men's room is crowded. Guys lined up at the urinals like we're in a wildly popular bar instead of a fast food shithole.

I'm sitting on the toilet, examining my fingernails and the bathroom is dead quiet except for regular bathroom sounds: flushing, paper towel dispenser, running water. No conversation going on at all. Just as it should be in a men's restroom.

Until:

-Fuck, man. You looking at my junk?

Someone makes a *tsk*ing sound.

-Don't flatter yourself, honey.

More quiet for a moment.

-Keep it up, fag. I'll end you.

This is sigh inducing and I really don't wanna be around when the fists start flying, so I get up and unlatch the stall's door.

The big tough guy is giving seething looks to a skinny dude with a pink Mohawk and a blue t-shirt emblazoned with the phrase 'this guy loves his boyfriend' and two thumbs pointing up to his face. The gay guy stares back at the redneck with an almost bored expression.

I'm trying to get by to get to the door when an older balding guy steps between the two other dudes, facing the gay guy.

-Have you heard the good news?

I pause on my way out, looking at them from over my shoulder. Is this shit really gonna happen?

The gay guy rolls his eyes.

-I know it by heart, but thanks for asking.

The redneck tosses his damp paper towel on the floor near the waste basket, drops the f word again and then shoves me aside to get out.

I bite my tongue. I'm at work after all.

The religious guy is still staring at the gay guy, smiling, holding out one hand as if he's gonna ask the dude to dance.

-Jesus forgives all sins.

-Good for Jesus.

Cracking up, I decide I might want to stay for this after all. These two are in the middle of a crowded bathroom, other guys moving around them as if they're inanimate objects inconveniently placed in the dead center of the room.

Most of them pretend they don't know what's going on but still, they start moving at a more leisurely pace.

The religious guy meets my gaze.

-Do you work here?

I want to say, good deduction, smart guy, the vest give it away? But I just nod.

He points at me.

-Tell this man about the righteous path to the Lord.

I frown.

-What?

Still pointing.

-Your necklace. You're catholic.

-Oh.

I touch the thin gold chain around my neck self-consciously. Hanging from it is a small crucifix.

-Nah. This was my mom's.

-But you're a believer, yes? You must be if your mother was.

This assumption is vaguely annoying to me for some reason.

-Not really. Sorry.

By now the dude with the Mohawk is going on his way, probably happy the focus has switched to me.

The balding guy's smile slips a notch.

-But this is a Christian establishment.

-It is?

-The owners support the bible's claim that marriage is between one man and one woman. How can you work here and not know that?

I shrug.

-Not sure where you're getting your info but this is the first I'm hearing of it.

His smile slips even further.

-Are you of the homosexual persuasion?

-What?

I'm quickly losing patience with this dude.

-Listen, nice chatting with you and all but I gotta get back to work.

-Does your boss know?

I take a deep breath and hold it for a couple seconds.

-Does he know what?

-About your persuasion. Isn't that what we're talking about here?

-Well, it's what *you're* talking about. A *lot*. And you know what they say about guys who talk about it a lot.

This earns me a few snickers from other guys in the john, but the religious dude goes from fake-friendly to pissed off in about half a second flat. I don't even realize right away that he's pulled a gun out from inside his jacket. Not until the other guys start shouting and scattering, bashing each other around to get out the door.

I see it just as my left shoulder explodes and the things that flash through my brain are startling.

I think about the headline: gun violence.

I think: thank Jesus I'm wearing my lucky underwear.

I think: hasn't this happened to me before? Was I shot? Or stabbed? What was it?

Then I hit the floor and I'm getting trampled

underfoot and I think: how fucking random. Figures this would happen to me.

I see the balding guy moving with the crowd, having dropped the gun, stepping over me.

Courteous, I think.

But seriously, hasn't this happened before? You'd assume I'd remember for sure something like this, but it's just not there in the front of my brain. So strange.

For the first time since the gun went off, all of fifteen seconds ago, I feel pain and with it comes a certainty. This has *definitely* happened before.

The four poster bed is such a cliché. I'm lying on a cloud. It's that comfortable.

I'm alone in the room but I can see beyond the windows that night has fallen once again and a mysterious someone has built a fire in the fireplace. A caring house elf perhaps?

Under the sheets, I've been stripped down to my underwear, which makes me wonder doubly who was in here but also makes me flash back to the spin.

He—*I*—had a pretty serious case of déjà vu right at the end there and it confuses me because I have the same sense. I've been shot before. Or stabbed, just like he thought.

Haven't I?

The bedroom door swings open and Luna enters carrying a tray. When she sees I'm awake, she looks startled but quickly recovers. She's good, this one.

-I brought you tea.

Sitting up on my elbows, I see she has. In a white china teapot decorated with little blue flowers with a matching cup and saucer.

-Tea? Really?

She sets the tray down on one of the nightstands.

-What's so strange about tea?

-Well, nothing, except that I haven't had it since I was about five years old and my grandmother made it for me. I thought it was impossible to get these days.

-Pretty close, but not quite impossible.

She sits on the red loveseat and crosses her legs.

There's an awkward moment when we just stare at each other. I struggle to come up with something to say.

-So…uh…so much for your two hour theory, huh?

-It *was* just a theory. Evidently, your brain is more susceptible to Satellite than most.

-What does that mean?

-You spin more frequently and, correct me if I'm wrong, you also have a stronger connection with the alternate versions of yourself.

-Stronger? How would I know that? I have nothing to compare it to.

-Granted. But *we* know that even if you don't.

-Then why did you say 'correct me if I'm wrong'?

-I assume your connections are growing stronger with each spin. Is that true?

I shrug.

-I have no idea. Maybe. But Atropos said they'll be stronger anyway, depending on the closeness of the other dimension.

-That's true. But it also depends on the strength of your brain activity.

Completely lost, I just look at her.

She uncrosses her legs and crosses them again. She thinks for a moment, maybe choosing her words carefully.

-You know how in old science fiction people were able to travel between dimensions by folding time and space, bringing the dimensions closer to each other so the journey would be shorter?

Now I really have no idea what she's talking about. I shake my head, afraid speaking will clue her in on my absolute ignorance of all things science related.

She continues, undeterred.

-Essentially, that's what happens in our brains.

Because, you see, our minds are infinite, just as the universe is infinite. Basically, we've discovered our minds *are* the universe. It's all the same thing. What's out there and what's in here.

She taps her temple with an elegant finger.

All at once it dawns on me that she, and possibly everyone in this house, could very well be crazy. What if they're just drug addicts who have finally fried their brains beyond all hope of repair? What if I've been inadvertently recruited into some bizarre drug cult? Maybe the spins are just what Harvey said they were: really intense trips caused by a new, extremely powerful hallucinogenic?

-You look worried.

I snap back to attention.

-Oh. No. I was just thinking about...umm...tea.

She cocks a thick blonde eyebrow at me.

-Tea?

-I'm really dying to try this tea. It smells...delicious.

Her expression becomes somewhat perplexed.

-I'm sure you can manage to pour yourself a cup.

-Oh...yeah. Yeah, of course I can.

I proceed to do just that, double checking that the covers don't fall below my waist in the process.

The tea is hot and good. Better than I remember. I take my time with multiple sips, smiling at Luna over the rim of the cup.

-Good.

-I'm glad you like it.

Unable to think of a response, I busy myself with downing the rest of the cup and pouring another.

Luna shifts her position.

-Do you want to talk about this later?

I'm stumped. Would it be rude to say I'd rather not talk about it at all? Of course it would, but that's the truth.

-Umm…do you know who…uh…undressed me?

-Circe.

Something like realization dawns on her face.

-I'm sorry. Are you uncomfortable? I can leave.

-Well, I was thinking…now that I've met Atropos, maybe I could go home. I'd really like a bath and a change of clothes and to, you know, brush my teeth. All that.

-I don't think—

A knock at the door interrupts her.

Now what? I think.

-Come in.

The door opens and a female guard pops her head in and addresses Luna.

-Atropos is asking for you.

Without hesitation, Luna rises from the sofa.

I sit up straighter in the bed.

-Wait. What about me?

Both women turn their attention to me as though I'm an afterthought.

-I'm sorry but you can't leave, Eon.

Luna doesn't *seem* sorry. At all.

-What do you mean? Like, *ever*?

-Not until you have your meeting with Atropos.

-I thought that already happened. Earlier.

Or was it yesterday? I can't be sure anymore. Time is all scrambled in my mind.

-Did she teach you how to control spinning?

-Uh…no? You were there, weren't you? She didn't teach me anything.

-She will.

-She will?

Luna nods.

-She taught me.

-Really?

The guard says Luna's name.

-I'll be back soon, Eon. In the meantime, the door to the right of the fireplace is a bathroom. You'll find everything you need in there.

-Oh. Okay. Cool. Thanks.

I feel like an idiot. I'd assumed it was a closet.

-But still, this whole 'I can't leave' thing—

-Please, Eon. We'll talk about it later.

Both women start to leave but I have one more question.

-But what if I…uh…spin again while you're gone?

-You've survived it on your own so far and unless I'm back in about…

She checks her watch.

-Ten minutes, I think it's a guarantee you will.

-Jesus!

-All the more reason for you to stick around and listen to what Atropos has to tell you.

She follows the guard out of the room and closes the door. I'm alone, my Adam's apple bobbing.

-Oh, crap.

Flipping the covers off myself, I jump out of bed and head to the bathroom, which makes me briefly flash on the last spin. The me who worked—*works?*—at a shitty Scrummy Burger.

I shove the memory out of my head. That part I'm getting pretty good at. I guess since the murder of my sister, I've become pretty fucking good at shoving things away that I don't want to think about, don't want to consider for even a single moment.

The bathroom, as expected, is amazing. The tub could probably fit four people comfortably. There are two sinks with large oval mirrors above them and everything is black marble and chrome. I touch the thickest, softest towel of my whole life and what's more is there's eight of them, not to mention matching wash cloths.

I could live in this bathroom with no complaints.

Remarkably, I decide to take a bath, though if you'd asked me yesterday, I would have sworn a nice hot shower would be enough for me to live happily ever after, considering my place in the city only has a tub and it basically sucks.

But now, as I watch this massive black bathtub fill with steaming water, I'm ready to dive in before it's a quarter full.

I strip out of my boxers and do just that, snatching up a bar of soap in the shape of a leaf and damned if it doesn't smell like a wild old forest. Or at least, what I imagine a wild old forest would smell like.

Noticing a bottle of bubble bath on a little shelf by the tub, I dump some into the water, giggling like a little kid.

Relaxing, the cool marble against my back a nice contrast to the hot water filling up around me, I can only think, *holy fuck, this is nice.*

I scrub myself, taking my time, playing with the fragrant bubbles and I develop a sense of satisfaction when it occurs to me that I've surely been in here much longer than ten minutes. So Luna was wrong.

The thought makes me chuckle. She strikes me as a woman who is seldom wrong and probably loathes it when she is.

My leisurely bath is so soothing I almost fall asleep but since I've always been paranoid about drowning in a tub, I force myself to get out when the water begins to grow tepid.

Another quick glance through the shelves by the sinks

and I find everything I need to shave, which I take advantage of as well.

When I'm finished, I wrap a towel around my waist and return to the bedroom in search of my clothes.

No clothes. Not in the dresser, not in the closet. Knowing these people, they're probably being washed. That's what rich people do for guests all the time in movies. Take their clothes away without asking and wash them.

I sit on the edge of the bed, debating on what I should do next. Go in search of someone or just wait? I was under the impression Luna would be back in just a few minutes and now it's got to be closer to an hour. Maybe longer.

I find myself wishing I had a watch but I don't. Never have. Who needs a watch when you don't even have a job?

Getting up from the bed, I go and poke at the fire, which is dying down now. With amusement, I wonder if there's a little bell I can ring for room service.

I imagine Circe dressed as my own personal butler and calling him Alfred. And naturally in my fantasy he calls *me* Master Eon.

Snickering, I sit down on the loveseat and then something tremendously bizarre happens:

I *feel* myself fall into a spin.

## CHAPTER SIXTEEN—The Rat

Dancing on a street corner wearing a rat costume isn't exactly my favorite way to spend a Friday morning, but what the hell. The money's not bad and it beats doing actual manual labor. Plus, the soda I bought from Scrummy Burger is laced with bourbon and it's sitting on the ground next to the sign which reads *A-Tat-Tat Extermination Services* and the phone number. The drink helps keep me motivated and I'm pretty sure it makes me a better dancer too.

I hop and spin and wiggle my hips, making punching motions with my arms, kicking out my legs and sometimes, for my own amusement, breaking into the chicken dance now and then.

The intersection I'm at is a busy one and I get a lot of catcalls, which I've learned to ignore. The nasty ones anyway. I also do a lot of waving, especially to little kids and pretty women when the cars on the street next to me have to stop for the light.

I've yet to collect a woman's phone number by doing some street flirting but I'm still hopeful. They can't see my face under this ridiculous rat head, but you never know. That might work to my benefit. Chicks don't care about looks as much as guys do anyway. With them, it's all about personality. I've found that if you can make a woman laugh, from there it's a very short stroll to the inside of her panties.

Even as I'm getting my groove on, with quick breaks to sip from the Scrummy Burger cup, I'm trying not to let the cold gray day depress me. I miss sunshine and warmth in the worst way.

The solution is to dance even harder, dance till I sweat and make the rat costume my own personal sauna.

A car full of teenagers stops at the light and the kid in the passenger seat rolls down his window and shouts at me, asking if I want some cheese.

Not the most original taunt I've ever received and certainly not worthy of a response.

He goes on from there, telling me to watch out for traps and cats and poison and finally the light changes and they take off, laughing uproariously at his lame jokes.

A black dude—most probably homeless by the looks of him—comes strolling up the sidewalk towards me. I'm kind of surprised to see he's smoking a pipe and the sweet scent of Virginia tobacco approaches me faster than he does.

I keep waving at the traffic and dancing my balls off for just over nine bucks and hour.

The guy stops walking when he reaches me, smiling and showing off an impressively large gap between his two front teeth, the stem of his pipe clenched tight in the side of his mouth.

He bobs his head in time with the non-existent music. My voice is muffled when I speak so I have to do so at a volume slightly louder than normal.

-How's it going, man?

He smiles wider and I suspect he's one of those sad souls who is not used to being acknowledged much.

-I like your dancing, rat man. It is full of joy and all the glory in Heaven.

*Oh boy*, I think. *Here we go again.*

-Thanks, my friend.

I don't know what else to say so why not just take it like the compliment it is?

The man pulls the pipe out of his mouth.

-You don't have to drink to celebrate the power of the Lord, you know.

-Uh huh.

I keep dancing for a couple seconds, vigorously, then I slow down. He can't see it but under my rat head, my eyes have gone wide.

-What?

Looking at the cup on the ground, then back at him. There's no point in denying anything. That's not really my style.

-How did you know?

The dude puffs out a thick cloud of tobacco smoke and laughs.

-Do you know who I am?

-Uh…nope.

-Take a guess.

-I have no idea who you are, my man. Should I?

-Hell, yes, you should! Look at me.

I do and notice his eyes shimmering with flecks of amber in the brown.

I decide to take a guess.

-You're Jesus, right?

He laughs again.

-You can't prove I'm not.

-True enough.

-That's why you should be kind to everyone you meet. You never know if he might really be Jesus. You believe that?

It doesn't take me long to think about it.

-Sure. I guess so.

-You guess so? You gotta do better than that, rat man. You gotta *know* so!

-Okay.

I do a spin and wave at the stopped traffic again.

He sucks on his pipe and watches me.

-You got the moves, son.

-Thanks.

Boogie boy could be my middle name. I should get a raise. Granted, I don't know how many customers A-Tat-Tat will get due to my epic dance skills, but I bet people will remember the name when and if they ever *do* need an exterminator.

My one man audience takes a couple steps to the side and kicks my drink over, spilling the contents onto the sidewalk.

I immediately stop dancing.

-What the fuck did you do that for?

-Just felt like it.

Speechless, I stare at him through the mesh eye holes in my rat head.

-You don't need that shit anyway, rat man. You got a light in you.

I groan loudly, feeling pretty agitated now. My attempts at a good mood despite this lousy weather have been for nothing.

-That wasn't cool, man.

He laughs heartily.

-You're the funniest rat man I ever did meet.

-That's terrific. I'm glad I could amuse you.

-And I do thank you for that.

He grins and I suspect he has no concept of sarcasm whatsoever.

-Unfortunately for you, rat man, I can see clear as day that you got a rider in your head.

I bend over and pick up my newly empty cup.

-I should make you buy me a new soda, but I bet you don't even have a dollar on you.

-Boy, you hear what I just said?

-Now I'm gonna have to wait till my next break before I can get another one. Lucky for you, I have the bottle of bourbon inside the building.

He takes a step closer to me, leaning into my rat face.

-You got a rider!

-What the fuck is a rider?

Backing up a bit, he examines his pipe, which has apparently burned out. Making a disgusted face, he looks up at me again.

-A rider is someone from another dimension getting ready to hijack your mind and once that happens, it's just a matter of time before they hijack your body and then—*BAM!*—your whole life.

-*Riiiight.* And you say I don't need to drink? I think I'm gonna call bullshit right now. It's you who doesn't need any more of…whatever it is you've been doing.

-I got the sight, rat man. I see your rider plain as you see me.

His eyes glitter gold as if catching sunlight, but there is no sunlight to catch.

Since I can't think of a response to that, I go back to dancing. Maybe I can burn off the frustration of having my beverage purposely spilled.

-Lucky for you, rat man, your ride is weak now. He'll move on and be stronger for some other poor bastard. I think you're safe.

-Oh, am I safe? That's good to know.

-This is no joke, rat man. Those riders are coming and I feel sorry for the ridees, if you get my drift.

I don't tell him that, no, I don't get his drift. Just keep dancing and waving, whipping my rattail around and around.

-You think I'm a crazy bum, don't you?

-I didn't say anything like that, man.

-You'll feel it when it starts to go down big time. It's already going down now but only certain people can see it.

I take a shot in the dark.

-People with the sight?

-That's right. And trust me, you won't wanna be buzzing on spirits when it happens. You're gonna need all your wits about you.

-Are you talking about the rapture or something like that? Armageddon?

-No, sir, rat man. Nothing like this was foretold in the good book. No, sir. More like Star Trek.

He laughs, just as jolly as you please, and pulls a tobacco pouch out from his coat pocket. He shakes a little bit into his pipe, puts it away and lights up with a wooden match he produces from nowhere and sparks up with his thumbnail.

After what seems like an extremely satisfying puff, he regards me with that smile again.

-You know, I bet you dance too fast for that rider you got. He can't get a good grip. Like riding a bucking bronco.

Something about the phrase 'bucking bronco' jars me, but I can't put my finger on why. I feel like maybe I recently had a dream where someone said the same thing.

-Goodbye, rat man.

He begins walking away and I can't decide if I'm happy or sad he's leaving me on the corner with only the passing traffic and depressing cloud cover to keep me company.

He crosses against the light, somehow manages to not get hit by a car and I turn away, dancing my heart out for the sake of extermination.

## CHAPTER SEVENTEEN—The Junkie (9)

I don't dream anymore. I only spin.

Sitting in what Atropos calls the parlor, a fire place large enough to park a small car within it giving off enough heat to make anyone forget winter has bought its ticket and is on the way, I tell her everything I can remember from all my different spins.

We're sitting across from each other in over-stuffed mint green chairs, a coffee table between us carved out of a huge oak log.

I'm drinking from a mug full of delicious vanilla coffee, anxious for this to be over.

Atropos is still intimidating, her albino-pale eyes so startling in her dark face, and her stillness, her complete absorption in what I'm saying.

I expect her to be surprised when I mention the man who could "see riders," but she nods placidly, letting me know this isn't the first time she'd heard of such a thing.

When I'm finished, she turns her attention to the fire, apparently lost in thought.

Nearly a minute passes, I finish my coffee, wondering if I'm being dismissed or what.

-This world is collapsing, Eon.

-Collapsing?

-There's not much good left beyond these walls. Soon—very soon—the human race will finish eating itself alive. We've already consumed everything we possibly could. I've heard stories of animals and clean oceans and forests where no man had ever walked, but all of these things ended before I was born.

I place my empty mug on the coffee table.

-There are still some animals.

-For how much longer? I have only seen photos of dogs. Dogs! They say there was once as many dogs as there were humans and I've never seen one. Nor have I seen many other animals, with the exception of rats. I suspect they'll be around much longer than we will. Once every tree has been chopped down and the only source of water comes from the sky, rats will somehow still thrive.

I think back on the rat man, dancing on a sidewalk while buzzed on bourbon.

-Rats get a bad rep. They're not so terrible.

Finally, she looks at me.

-I suppose there is much to admire about them, yes. And much to emulate. We need to adapt to save ourselves, Mr. Eon. And do you know how we can do that?

The man with the golden flecks in his eyes flashes in my mind but I shake my head.

-We have to spin ourselves into another world and pray the one we land in is in better shape than this one.

I shift in my chair.

-Not sure I follow.

-It's just like the man with the pipe told you. We will, for lack of a better description, have to upload our consciousness into our parallel selves. The trick will be to not end up in a dimension worse than the one we currently occupy, such as when you were digging in rubble and reminiscing about dog food.

-But...that sounds...I don't know. Unfair.

-To who?

-Our...parallel selves. How can we just...take over their bodies? Their lives?

-Don't think of it as taking over. Think of it as more

of a melding.

I say nothing and it's clear she can read the apprehension on my face. For all I know, she can read my mind.

-Mr. Eon, you needn't worry about them. They'll only be aware of us for a very brief amount of time and then they'll forget anything was ever...unusual about that day.

I'm still more than a little skeptical.

-How do you know?

For the first time, she smiles ever so slightly.

-I know.

-You've tried it before?

-In a manner of speaking, yes.

The parlor doors open and Luna walks in. She seems surprised to see me before addressing Atropos.

-I went back to Hoop's bar like you asked, but I couldn't find any Satellite. They must have taken it with them.

Atropos gets to her feet abruptly and there's no mistaking her emotion—she's pissed.

-Where could they have taken it?

Luna shrugs.

-Not sure but Circe is still out there searching for them. I think if we find Hoop without Halleck there's a good chance he'll tell us. But if he's still with Halleck...

She trails off, looking distressed, like she's expecting a severe punishment.

Atropos's eyes darken a shade.

-This is exactly why I told you to grab it when you rescued Mr. Eon.

-But there wasn't time. You said not to—

-Kill them, yes.

Atropos walks to the fireplace and stares at the flames as if she's gazing into a crystal ball.

-We can't allow them to sell Satellite as if it's a common street drug. You know how selective we have to be. If it gets into the wrong hands...

She turns back, glancing at me and I have to wonder if I'm an example of 'the wrong hands.'

I clear my throat and stand up.

-Maybe I should get out of your hair. Let you two have some privacy.

-Sit down.

Atropos commands without raising her voice.

I do as I'm told, growing increasingly uncomfortable. In fact, I'm starting to wonder why I'm in this house at all and really, who the fuck are these people? Why did I just go along for the ride unquestioningly?

Luna gives me a sympathetic look. It's as if we're siblings getting scolded by our mother, who is, incidentally, far younger than we are, and we're not even sure what we did wrong.

Atropos fixes her attention on Luna once more.

-What are the chances Hoop will be with Halleck?

-I'm not sure.

Luna appears as if she's feeling a tremendous amount of guilt for not knowing the correct answer and I can't help but feel bad for her.

I decide to pipe in.

-Hoop and I used to hang out sometimes when we were younger. There's a cemetery near his bar and we'd go in there sometimes to get high and drink. We took girls in there once in a while when we got older. There were vaults and shit. Locks smashed off. It was creepy I guess but we were kids. We thought it was cool.

When Luna speaks, her voice is tinged with doubt.

-That might have been a good place for children to hide, but grown men would—

Atropos holds up a hand in a stop gesture and Luna's mouth snaps shut. Atropos studies me intently.

-How good is your memory of this cemetery?

I'm puzzled by this question but answer honestly.

-Pretty good. To tell you the truth, it hasn't been long since the last time I was there. Hoop stopped going there when we grew up but I...

I feel like an idiot but plunge forward anyway.

-I never totally stopped. If I happened to be closer to the cemetery than to where I lived and I had drugs on me...

Atropos nods and moves around the coffee table to stand directly in front of me. When she sits on the table, she holds her hands out to me, palms up.

Luna comes forward, alarmed.

-Atropos, I don't think—

-Quiet. Mr. Eon, please take my hands and close your eyes. I want you to focus all your thoughts on the cemetery. Every tiny detail that comes to you, bring it forth.

-But...why?

Her eyes on mine, beseeching, so close to pictures I've seen of frozen ponds.

-Have you ever heard of remote viewing?

-I...yeah, but...

I blink.

-I thought it was like...sci-fi bullshit. Something they did on that old show The X-files and shit like that.

She remains still, hands in the same open position.

-Please.

I glance once at Luna, who helps not one iota.

Finally, I take a breath and do as Atropos has instructed, taking her hands in mine, closing my eyes and remembering the cemetery.

I'm not sure what I'm expecting to feel. A jolt maybe? Something violent. But what comes is more of a tickling sensation, as if a tiny mite is casually strolling across the surface of my brain, its miniscule feet barely detectable but at the same time, wholly present.

Concentrating on the landscape of the cemetery, I see myself slipping between two mysteriously bent wrought iron bars in the ancient fence surrounding the land. I see the old and crumbling tombstones, the gnarled trees, so spooky and somehow wonderful against a night sky, the sarcophagus I lost my virginity on and further back, the four tombs we used to go inside and smoke, shoot, snort or drop whatever we'd managed to score that day.

Inside the largest, I see the dead leaves shoved into the corners by unfriendly winds, wrappers of various sorts, an old soda can, someone's discarded knit hat, old works and a few used condoms.

From there, I remember the other tombs, though we hadn't used them as often and though they were smaller, nowadays their interiors were much the same. A single sarcophagus in each.

Another scan of the cemetery grounds and I can't think of anything else I may have missed.

When I open my eyes, I discover Atropos has already opened hers. She lets go of my hands and straightens her back.

-Well? Did it work? Did you see my memories?

-I saw what you think are your memories but in actuality is how the cemetery looks now.

I press my lips together, trying to comprehend, but the truth is I can't and by the time I'm ready to ask her to explain the statement, she's risen from her spot on the table and is talking to Luna again.

-Hoop's not there.

-He must be with Halleck then.

-Maybe.

Atropos returns her attention to me, about to say something and then I notice her eyes widen a fraction. When she speaks, it's actually to Luna.

-He's going again.

## CHAPTER EIGHTEEN—The Soldier

If there's any one good thing about being confined to a wheelchair it's that I'm on the perfect eye level to check out women's asses and they can't bitch about it too much. That doesn't mean no one ever has bitched about it-one woman damn near slapped me once, but that's probably more because I was drunk and got belligerent when she confronted me about staring at her butt.

Every time I tell anyone about that story, I crack up. I realize you had to be there, but damn, it was funny.

This convention hall is crowded as all fuck, but, hey, guy in a wheelchair, mofos. Coming through.

They make a path in the same way traffic pulls to the side of the road when a police cruiser with a wailing siren races by.

Which is also kind of funny because the one cop I've ever known personally told me once that half the time they're driving around like that, they're speeding through town to go get a pizza or some shit. Apparently they think it's funny to watch everyone nearly kill themselves to get to the right side of the road.

When he told me that I was half, what a douche bag, and half, that is fucking awesome.

I'm sometimes tempted to imitate a siren myself when I'm in a crowd like this but I refrain. Most people are nice enough and move without complaint. And even on the rare occasion when they don't get out of the way, my wife has been known to give them hell on my behalf.

Not that I'm incapable of giving someone hell—I've doled out more than my share—but when she does it…well, I have to admit it's pretty hot.

She's twelve years my junior and has more moxie in her pinky finger than I have in my whole body. And I'm pretty spunky myself.

-Look over there, Jeff!

I follow her finger and see what's excited her so much: a booth where a couple of the actors from one of her favorite horror movies, *The Blood Room*, are signing eight by ten glossies of themselves and, from the looks of it, maybe posing for pictures with fans as well.

Her grin makes me grin.

-Let's do it. The line isn't too long yet.

She does a little excited hop and leads the way. I roll after her, checking out a few nicely rounded female butts along the way.

This is the third or fourth horror convention we've been to and we've learned to get here early, but even so, tons of people have gotten here even earlier, so the rows between booths are still pretty crowded, but not as bad as they will be an hour or two from now.

Once we're in line to meet the actors from the movie, the couple in front of us turn around, smiling.

-Isn't this awesome?

The woman, clearly in her forties but dressed like someone two decades younger, beams at me and my wife in turn. The hazel eyes behind her black-framed glasses look almost delirious with joy.

In unison, my wife and I agree it is indeed awesome.

The man, also in his forties, but maybe creeping towards the big five-oh, puts his arm around the woman and nods. He's a big dude—over six feet by at least a few inches—and he looks like a musician in a heavy metal band with his long, dark hair, a bushy beard streaked with gray that almost reaches his chest and muscular arms with full tattoo sleeves. The tats, I notice, are mostly of colorful demons and other supposedly scary imagery.

Looking down at me, he offers me his fist, which I bump without question. Horror fans are almost always instantaneous family.

After the bump, he asks what so many always do.

-You a vet?

-Yep.

-Thanks for everything you do, man. You're a true American hero.

The woman agrees heartily.

-Yes! Thank you so much!

She reaches down and squeezes my forearm with affection.

-Is it okay to ask what happened?

This is not my favorite subject by a long shot but I understand people are curious. Not a lot actually come out and ask but some do, so I have a well-rehearsed answer prepared.

-Shrapnel in the back. Spine injury. But hey, honorably discharged and I was only over there for three months. Almost makes it worth it.

This isn't even close to true. It was most definitely *not* worth it, but people always dig a positive attitude so it's my standard reply. No point in making people feel shitty.

My wife, who knows all this, jumps in and saves the day, as she often does.

-How many times have you guys seen *The Blood Room?* It's a Halloween tradition in our house.

The two give each other considering looks before the guy answers.

-I'd say going on twenty. The special effects blow my fucking mind every time. I'm a special effects buff. Done a little myself.

-No shit?

I'm not just pretending to be impressed. I genuinely am, as I've had a few aspirations towards filmmaking myself.

-Yeah, man. I worked on *The Screamers*. You ever heard of that one?

-Sorry, no. Is it online?

-Sure is. And DVD too, but you have to go to the website to order it. Blood Death Films. Local company. I've done a bunch of shit for them. Even acted in a few.

-We both have.

The guy's wife—at least I assume they're married— puts in.

-I've done more acting than he has.

-I've written a couple screenplays too.

He keeps talking as if his wife hasn't said a word.

-Hoping to be a director.

I bob my head.

-That rocks. I wouldn't mind doing that myself.

The line moves forward and we're closer to the table. It's slow going though, because people want to linger with the actors, thinking the longer they chat, the more like friends they'll become. The actors will remember them next time they meet. Hopefully. And you never know what an actor—even a ninth tier actor—can do for you somewhere down the line.

The bearded man keeps talking.

-I have a screenplay called *The Haunting of Petunia Stewart* that Ron Zuko—he's the head of Blood Death— is reading now. Fingers crossed, you know?

-Yeah? That's fucking awesome, man. Congrats.

We do the thumb-grab hand shake while both of our women look on, nodding and smiling.

The line moves forward again and we're that much

closer to the actors. We can almost hear what they're saying to the fans, but not quite.

Suddenly, there's a shout of alarm and one of the actors leaps up and away from the table, his arms pinwheeling madly as he struggles to keep his balance, the chair he was seated in falling over and tripping him up from behind.

The actor seated next to him also stands up, one hand placed against his throat and blood spurting out from between his fingers to spatter his white dress shirt and the table top in front of him.

Another man leans over the front of the table holding what looks like a box-cutter, both it and his hand slicked red.

The people closest to the table scatter every which way while those of us further back look on with something like fascination.

The metal guy with the beard and tattoos barks a laugh.

-Holy shit! Too fucking cool!

People moving around block my view of the chaos unfolding in front of us and I, like many others, at first assume it's a publicity stunt taken right out of the plot of *The Blood Room*, wherein the characters converge in a room where all their throats are sliced open by a demonic entity which grows stronger with each kill.

Judging by some of the reactions from the people closer to the table than we are, I suspect them to be plants—other actors, playing along with this little bit of live theater.

And I have to admit, they're really good. Better than the actors who were signing the photos, that's for sure. Some of the crowd run off screaming as if they'd witnessed an actual murder take place, passing security racing towards the signing booth.

Also actors, of course. Either that or they were previously told about this stunt and they're just being good sports and playing along.

They're not as talented as the fleeing 'cast,' though. They're too grim, as if maybe they're biting the insides of their cheeks to keep from laughing.

The 'murderer' flings himself over the top of the table and on top of the fallen actor, disappearing from my line of sight, which wasn't too great to begin with.

The other actor is already long gone. Probably in the damn parking lot by now, thankful he isn't stuck inside anymore, maybe having a smoke while he chuckles at the stunt he and his comrades have just pulled, scaring people who should really know better.

I laugh at the commotion and look at my wife.

-You'd think these people had never seen *Kiss of Blood*, wouldn't you?

She turns away from the hysteria playing out in front of us.

-Huh?

-Well, obviously Steve Moody isn't dead since he's in the sequel to *The Blood Room*. I mean, I know it sucks but still...I don't see how anyone is even falling for this.

Her blank expression confuses me.

-I know we only saw *Kiss of Blood* a couple times, babe, but you're looking at me like...

I stop, confused by what I'm saying. There's an abrupt pain in my head, right behind my eyes and all at once, I'm not feeling so great. Like I might puke. I cough, covering my eyes with my hand.

When I drop my hand I see that up ahead of us, people have started laughing, while one or two others are cursing, unamused by the little act just played out in front of them.

The actor with the supposedly sliced throat stands up, his hand clasped with that of his potential murderer, both of them grinning from ear to ear, pleased with their own performances.

The big tattooed guy turns to look at me again.

-Did I hear you say there's gonna be a sequel to *The Blood Room*?

I open my mouth to tell him, no, there already *is* a sequel to it, but there isn't, so my mouth closes again and I'm thinking back to the battlefield. The gunfire. The screaming. The blood and the death.

I haven't suffered a head injury, then or ever. So why...

Still thinking about *Kiss of Blood*, a movie which doesn't exist—at least not yet—I spin my wheelchair around and begin heading for the exit to this ridiculously large, loud, crowded room. I need to find a restroom, pronto, and I don't stop for anything, not even the sound of my wife's voice calling after me.

I was pretty good at disregarding the spins before but I'm getting even better at it. I barely ponder the me in the wheelchair at all when I come out of it.

Still in the parlor, still in the same chair, I look around and, though the light is slanted across the ceiling differently, it's the only discernable variation in the room. The fire still burns bright in the fireplace and Atropos and Luna are still here, both seated on a sofa nearby.

Luna raises an eyebrow at me.

-Welcome back.

I lean forward in my chair, rub at my eyes. Coming out of a spin is not unlike waking up from a deep sleep and carrying a very vivid dream out of it with you. There doesn't seem to be any of the ugly side effects that often come with drug use and for this much, I'm grateful.

-Were you close?

I stop rubbing my eyes to see Atropos watching me placidly.

-Huh?

-Did the alternate you sense your presence?

-I…maybe. He had a memory. A memory of mine. I guess the timeline is a little different where he's from. I think he thought it was more of a premonition than anything else.

-And his world? Was it intact?

-I think so, yeah. But…I mean, he was inside a building, so I don't know for sure. But it seemed fine. People were happy.

-Your spins are more frequent than anyone else I've

ever encountered. It's going to make training you difficult.

-Training me?

Luna is equally baffled.

-Training him? But he's only been spinning for less than a week. I spun for—

-Quiet.

Atropos glares at Luna momentarily.

-Now is not the time for pettiness, Luna. We need to find our revolver and Mr. Eon is the closest we've come to a contender.

-That's not true! I'm already trained!

-You are.

Atropos places a hand on Luna's knee.

-But Mr. Eon is the fastest I have ever seen. He's barely back from one spin before he begins the next. It's unprecedented.

-Is he faster than me?

All of our heads swivel to the doorway to see Hoop standing there, holding a gun to Circe's head.

Even though the sight of this doesn't seem to overly alarm the women, I leap to my feet and scramble backwards, ready to dive behind furniture if the barrel even looks like it might swing towards me.

Atropos rises, her head slightly tilted to one side.

-Yes, even faster than you, Mr. Hooper.

I didn't think it would be possible, but it is. And the most amazing part of it is, Mr. Eon doesn't even try. It's as though his brain was malleable even before his first dose of Satellite.

Hoop's face darkens.

-That's because he's a fucking junkie! What part of that do you not get? He's not reliable! *I* was the one who was supposed to lead us out of here! *You* told me that!

Despite Hoop screaming at her, Atropos doesn't flinch.

-I'm sorry, Mr. Hooper. I was mistaken. At the time, I never imagined someone could be faster, but here he is. And you're the one responsible for him.

-No, I'm not! It was that stupid fuck Dent! He's the one to blame, not me!

-And you took care of him, didn't you?

My face is beaded with sweat, as is Circe's. In fact, the guy is struggling not to cry and I'd bet my last fix he's gonna piss his pants any second.

Even Luna, standing next to Atropos, appears a bit nervous. And if not nervous, then at least *concerned*.

But Atropos takes another step towards Hoop and continues to talk calmly.

-I think you should put the gun down, Mr. Hooper. We can talk this out.

-*No!*

Hoop shrieks, removing the muzzle of the gun from the back of Circe's head and pointing it at Atropos.

-We already fucking talked, Atropos! Or don't you remember? You said I was too erratic. Remember that? Well, how's this for fucking erratic? All the spins in the world and you didn't see this coming, did you?

Atropos regards Hoop the way an especially patient teacher would study a child throwing a tantrum.

-Do you think you can shoot me, Mr. Hooper?

Instantly, Atropos falls to the floor and my first thought was that, yes, Hoop did think he could shoot her and in fact, did.

But then Hoop...changes. The fire goes out of his eyes and they adopt that same calm tranquility Atropos's eyes possess. He steps forward and hands the gun to Luna, who puts it into the back of her waistband under her leather jacket.

Circe falls to his knees, repeating the word

-*Fuck!*

over and over again.

I'm inclined to agree with him.

-What the fuck just happened?

I look at Atropos, still unmoving on the floor.

Hoop turns robot-like and leaves the room.

-Holy shit! What the fuck?

Yes, I'm repeating myself, but...

Luna bends down to examine Atropos, pressing two fingers to her throat.

I join her on the other side of the body.

-Is she dead?

Luna glances at me and I'm stunned to see her smiling. Not a lot. Just a corner of her mouth tugging upwards as if on a string. But a smile just the same.

-No, she's not dead. She'll rejoin us in a minute.

-What? Rejoin us? What in the holy shit does that mean?

Atropos blinks, startling the crap out of me and making me fall back onto my ass.

Luna's smile grows.

-This is 'what in the holy shit' that means.

Sitting up, Atropos looks at me.

-I'm sorry to have scared you, Mr. Eon. Sometimes a little leap is a necessary evil.

-A little...leap? You mean, you...you...

-I leaped into Mr. Hooper, yes.

Luna helps her to her feet.

-He is safely locked in the library down the hall. He'll sleep for some time to come.

-But...how? How did you do it?

She offers me a hand and when she pulls me to my

feet, I'm astounded by her strength. She is definitely not your average seventeen year old girl.

-I just craft a mind bridge.

She says this like it's something I should know already. Like it's something everyone knows already.

Walking over to where Circe is still on the floor, she pulls him up with the same ease she did me before glancing at Luna.

-How much time?

Luna looks at me, then back to her and shakes her head.

-Not much. It's faster and faster now. Two minutes. Maybe.

Atropos scowls, a barely detectable change in her brow.

-That's not enough time.

-Not even close.

Luna tells me to sit down.

-Why?

She sighs.

-Why do you even question anymore? Haven't you seen enough?

She has a point. I sit.

Atropos sits on the table again, just as she did earlier.

-Déjà vu.

-Indeed. Take my hands again, please, Mr. Eon.

I do as I'm told.

Her hands are warm and soft. She doesn't have to tell me to close my eyes this time. I just do it, feeling more and more like a trained monkey.

-I'm coming with you this time, Mr. Eon.

My eyes fly open.

-*What?* You can do that?

-I can.

-Then why didn't you do it before?

-Because it's dangerous.

-Dangerous? Am I going to get hurt?

-No. Not dangerous for you. Dangerous for them.

-Oh. Well…still. That seems bad.

-And dangerous for me.

Now I'm the one scowling.

-That's even worse!

I yank my hands away.

She reaches for them again.

-It's necessary.

-Why?

-You'll see.

Luna crosses the room to stand beside us.

-I don't think this is a good idea, Atropos.

I nod.

-It's a terrible idea. And besides, hasn't it already been two minutes? I think Luna called this one wrong. No offense, Luna. But I really feel fine. I don't think I'll be spinning anytime soon. I'm actually kind of hungry. When was the last time I ate?

Atropos holds my hands in a death grip. I don't think I could pull away even if I used all my strength, which is pretty unnerving. Her eyes remain closed and she gives no indication she's heard a word I've said.

Circe comes over and sits on the sofa behind her. His eyes are red and watery and even though I think he's a douche, I avert my gaze, feeling kind of bad for the dude.

Luna, however, has no such qualms.

-And you! How the hell did you manage to let Hoop get the upper hand on you? Where was he? Where's Halleck?

-Not now.

Atropos interrupts Luna, her voice a lower octave than

normal.

-When Mr. Eon and I return we will discuss this at length.

I'm still mystified by everything but for just a moment the fog clears and I see the truth as clearly as I can see Atropos's face.

-You're not human, are you?

The question doesn't faze her in the slightest.

-Of course not.

## CHAPTER TWENTY—The Woman

I'm having another spaz attack and it's no joke. There is simply not enough time in the day for me to be able to make my deadline. No matter that the deadline is self-imposed. I take this shit seriously and if I'm not finished with this book in a week I may as well just give it all up. And that means, no more writing.

But who the fuck am I kidding? I'll write no matter what. It's what I'm driven to do, even if no one ever reads it but me, and let's face it, I have manuscripts that even I don't ever want to read again and this current one could very well be included in that sad, sorry group.

Time to buck up and make more coffee.

I can do this.

Once I have a fresh mug of espresso, I return to my desk and read over the last few paragraphs of my latest paranormal romance novel featuring vampires, tentatively titled *Night of Dread*.

This is my third novel featuring the same characters and I'm looking forward to selling the series to a major publisher once I'm finished with this last one. Ha. That was a joke, of course. But, hey, I can dream.

The cursor blinks at me and I'm reminded of a heart monitor in a hospital. If it's still blinking, I'm alive, yes?

A sip of coffee and I set the mug down, cracking my knuckles. I begin to type, moving gracefully to the next part of the story without a hitch. Being such an anal outliner, I'm able to finish my novels at a speed most writers envy and I'm approaching the climax of the book so my enthusiasm makes me go that much faster.

But the next time I pause for more coffee, I look at what I'm doing and the enthusiasm is suddenly gone.

*This isn't what I should be doing right now. I need to go outside.*

A quick glance at the clock on the wall tells me it's almost 9 PM but that's irrelevant. I push my desk chair back and leave my office, part of my mind knowing I forgot to hit save on my work in progress, hoping there isn't a power surge and I lose my work, but that's not important right now.

I'm driven to find out what's happening in the world.

In the living room, my husband is on the sofa, curled beneath a blanket and watching a crime show on television. The rest of the room is dark and blue ghosts chase each other across the walls, shadows cast by the TV.

He looks up at me with surprise.

-Hey. You're out early.

It's true. I have a strict schedule. Every night I'm in my office writing from eight to eleven, no exceptions, and I'm not to be disturbed for any reason except a dire emergency and as far as I'm concerned, there are no emergencies dire enough.

-I'm going out.

I pass through the living room and into the kitchen. Part of me knows I should be grabbing a coat—last I knew, it was only 32 degrees outside—but I don't bother. I open the door and step out into the night, walk down the stoop and out to the sidewalk, ignoring the car completely.

-Honey?

My husband again, calling after me from the open door.

-Are you okay?

I can't be bothered to reply. I'm looking around the

neighborhood, at each house I pass, the sky, the traffic.

There's nothing unusual about anything. Just a quiet autumn night in Berlin where I came to live with the man I married after I got my surgery.

He's a good man, indifferent to the fact that I was born a man myself, but…it just wasn't right. I always knew it wasn't right and though I've had some tough relationships, Scott just got it right away. He understood. Or at least he seemed to. He didn't judge me for it. Told me he loved me. That was nice.

He's coming after me now, calling me by name, but I can't think about him at this moment. I have to take in the night.

Berlin.

Such an extraordinary city. Such history here. So different from Alabama where I grew up, always getting called a faggot, even though I knew it wasn't true. No one believed me. Not even my family. It took moving away to New York for me to finally get the courage to do what I knew needed to be done.

-Jess! Where are you going? Will you please stop for a minute?

Scott grabs my arm and spins me around. He looks scared and he's still in his bare feet, wearing just sweats and a t-shirt, just like me. We're both in our comfy night clothes.

He demands an answer from me.

-*Where are you going? What's wrong?*

-I have to see it.

-See what?

I think about the question for a minute but it's so all encompassing, so hard to grasp.

-Everything.

I pull my arm away and continue on with my

exploration but he is not easily dissuaded. He follows, almost jogging to keep up because I'm walking so fast. Much faster than my usual pace.

-Everything looks okay here.

It does and for some reason this pleases me. I don't know what I was expecting, but it was...something. War, maybe? Famine? Destruction of some kind. A world in ruins.

Why would I think that? Did I have a nightmare? Maybe I'm dreaming right now. It certainly feels like it could be a dream. I'm tired and feel spacey, not sure where I'm going but still with a burning need to get there.

-Jess!

My husband is shouting now, and people will probably begin to take notice, which I can't let happen. I stop and turn to him.

-Everything is fine, Scott. Go back home. I'll return shortly.

His gray eyes widen.

-You'll return *shortly*? Where are you going? It's freezing out here.

-I need to check on something.

-What?

I ponder it, but don't have an answer for him, which is strange. What do I need to check on?

-Stop following me.

Even I'm surprised at the harshness in my voice but I don't have time to think about it. I keep going down the street, observing everything I can.

Nothing is out of the ordinary. All is peaceful. But this is such a small part of one city and there is an entire world to think about. I need to find a reliable news source. Should I go back to the house and watch TV?

I sniff the cold air and pay attention to how it feels in

my lungs. Everything is important—even the smallest detail.

Walking for several blocks, completely absorbed in my study of the environment, I barely notice when a police car pulls up alongside me.

Two police officers emerge, as well as my husband. One of the cops stops me by blocking my path. He says something in German but my German isn't very good.

My husband's German however, is outstanding, and he starts talking to the officers. He gestures at me a lot and both the cops are watching me as if I might suddenly do something irrational.

I interrupt them all.

-Is walking at night illegal?

They ignore me, so I repeat the question, much louder.

*-Is walking at night illegal?*

Scott and the one officer, the older of the two, stop talking finally.

-You know it's not illegal, Jess.

My husband says.

-But you're going to freeze. And why won't you just tell me what's going on? Is this research for your book?

Good, I think. Very good.

-Yes, I'm researching for my book.

-Well, why didn't you just say that? Why didn't you get dressed and put on a coat? What's gotten into you? You know I would have come with you if you'd just asked.

-But it's not necessary for you to come with me. Unless…

Why am I being so stupid?

The truth is, I'm not sure exactly what I'm doing or what I'm hoping to find or not find.

The older cop says something to me in German and gestures towards the police car.

Scott translates for me.

-He's offering us a ride home.

I shiver and wrap my arms around myself, realizing that, like Scott, I'm not dressed for a cold night walk.

What the hell is wrong with me?

I allow myself to be escorted into the back of the police car, Scott climbing in after me.

There is a lot of talk between the officers and my husband, but since I can't understand hardly anything they're saying, I tune them out and gaze at the passing scenery.

When we arrive back at the house and go inside, Scott tells me the cops believed I was on drugs and there was nothing he could say to convince them otherwise.

-They also asked me if we've been fighting. They wanted to know if I'd hit you.

I sit down at the kitchen table and realize my hands are trembling but I don't think it's because of the cold. The fact is, I *do* feel drugged. Overly caffeinated perhaps. My mind is racing, flittering from one topic to the next, wondering about the economy of all things, the state of world politics, who is fighting with who, which country is on the verge of economic collapse, how powerful is the United States?

I grip my head in both hands and scream, scaring not only myself but Scott as well. He turns away from the cupboard where he was getting down mugs for tea, dropping one to the floor where it shatters.

-It's too tight! Loosen it!

The words coming out of my mouth make no sense to me, but I yell them anyway.

-Loosen your grip!

Squeezing my eyes shut, I begin to sob. I'm terrified. I don't know why my emotions are not aligning with my words and thoughts. Is this what going crazy means? Were my asshole parents, so homophobic and racist and nasty, right all along? Am I mentally ill?

And that's the most painful of all. What if they were right?

What if I truly am an insane abomination?

# CHAPTER TWENTY-ONE—The Junkie (11)

In the parlor again. Or still. Whatever.

-Well, that sucked.

Atropos's face tells me she agrees, though she doesn't say anything.

-Not only did it suck but it was fucking weird. I was a transwoman. What the hell?

Circe, apparently already recovered from his brush with death, snorts.

-Did you feel yourself up? Man, if I had tits, I'd never leave the house.

-Christ. Shut up, man.

Luna, standing by the fireplace with her arms crossed, looks at Atropos.

-Any luck?

-It seemed fine.

Atropos gets to her feet and stretches.

-I need to lie down for a while.

She exits the room, the three of us silent until the door closes behind her.

Still smiling, Circe nods at me with his chin.

-How did you like your first ride along?

-Are you deaf? I said it sucked. That... woman... thought she was going crazy. Atropos was... I don't know... steering her, I guess.

Luna nods.

-That's the point.

-But what was she looking for?

-A suitable dimension. You're really not very bright, are you?

Telling her to fuck off is on the tip of my tongue but I hold back. She's pretty hot and if I've learned anything at all about women in my years on planet earth, it's that they don't take kindly to being told to fuck off.

Instead, I stand up.

-I'm starving. Is there anything to eat in this joint?

Circe does his standard chuckle.

-He gets to ride with Atropos and he's hungry. Dude. I have never gotten to ride with her. You have to give us more details than 'it sucked.'

-There are no more details. It was weird and kind of scary, like being on a runaway train or something. It wasn't a good experience.

Luna starts for the door.

-I'm pretty hungry myself. We should eat and then check on Hoop. Maybe by now he's had a change of heart and will be willing to tell us more about Halleck.

I run a hand through my hair, following her out of the room and towards the kitchen.

-Why doesn't Atropos just...uh...possess him? Dig around in his brain to find out about Halleck?

She shrugs.

-I don't know. Maybe she already has. Or maybe Hoop doesn't know where Halleck is. Or at least, he doesn't know he knows.

Bringing up the rear, Circe is hurrying to catch up to us.

-I have a good mind to skull fuck him with the fucking gun he put to my head.

As we enter the kitchen, I shouldn't be amazed by the size of it, given the rest of the mansion, but I am just the same. Everything is state of the art and unlike anything I've ever encountered before. Shiny and new. In other words, nothing like the world I'm used to.

Luna opens the refrigerator.

-What do you guys feel like having?

Joking around, I peer over her shoulder into the appliance.

-Where's Pennyworth?

-Who?

-Never mind.

She clearly doesn't care enough to question me further.

-Vegetable stew it is.

Seated at the horseshoe shaped counter, Circe groans.

-I need meat, woman.

-Then make your own damn food.

He sighs heavily, as if the weight of the world is on his shoulders.

-Luna here doesn't eat meat, so we can't either.

Luna turns to him.

-Do you know how few animals are left? If it wasn't for selfish pricks like you there might be more.

He doesn't react until she turns away and then, making a show of it, he gives the finger to her back.

I clear my throat.

-Well, at least I've joined a nice big happy family.

-You haven't joined shit.

Circe's face is no longer amused.

-You have to prove yourself worthy.

-Atropos thinks he's worthy.

Luna's words give me a slight satisfaction, even though she pretty much called me a dumbass not five minutes ago. I'm beginning to think she thinks all guys are douchebags, which doesn't bode well for me and my nefarious intentions towards her.

To make up for it, I offer to help her make our meal, which she accepts. Circe disappears for a while, saying he'll be back soon, and I wonder if he's going to pay a visit to Hoop but ultimately I think he might be a bit too cowardly to do it on his own.

While I'm chopping vegetables at the counter, I figure now is as good a time as any to try and get a better feel for Luna.

-So, Luna. You got a boyfriend?

She gives me a quick smirk but I can't tell if it's real or she's being sarcastic.

-Don't be an idiot, Eon.

I let that sit for a second, but only a second.

-A girlfriend?

-I'm holding a sharp object.

She warms me, but I sense she's just being playful. At least, I hope she's just being playful.

I decide to press my luck, regardless.

-If you had to choose between a boyfriend and a girlfriend, which would it be?

She puts down the knife she's using to do her own chopping and glowers at me.

-How's this for an answer? If you think you have a single prayer in the world of having a shot at me, you will go to your grave a very disappointed man.

I raise a brow at her.

-So…girlfriend, then?

-I'm not kidding, Eon. Drop it.

-Fine.

Under my breath, I do a little muttering.

-Shit. Just an innocent question. Making conversation.

We prepare the rest of the meal in silence, as I'm pretty sure I've managed to piss her off and I'm even more sure she could easily kick my ass if she wanted to, judging by the way she busted me out of the basement at Sennacherib's.

When it's time to eat, we move into a dining room that seems like it's from a different era than the kitchen. While the kitchen was uber modern, the dining room is more 19th century chic. Decorated in hues of blue and bronze with elegant arched windows, it is the airiest of the rooms I've been in so far.

The windows look out on the western grounds and far in the distance, mountain peaks can be seen just over the tops of the bordering forest.

Circe must have been able to smell the food because he enters a minute after it's been placed on a table large enough to seat ten people quite comfortably.

-I'm ready to get my veggie on!

He helps himself to a bowl and begins serving the stew to himself, sniffing it loudly.

My stomach grows mightily and I realize just how hungry I am. All this spinning throughout the galaxy can evidently work up a person's appetite.

It has been a long time since I ate fresh vegetables and I say as much after the first spoonful.

Luna smiles and for once I don't doubt it's genuine.

-There's a greenhouse on the property and we have a very good gardener.

-And lots of guards guarding the gardener.

Circe laughs at his joke with his mouth full.

Ignoring him, Luna tells me I should probably eat fast.

This is not welcomed news.

-Fuck. Am I gonna spin again?

-I give you less than an hour, tops. Probably closer to forty-five minutes.

-Fucking-A!

I'm starting to get really pissed off about this shit. I don't even get a high from it. I get nothing but a headache and I still haven't gotten back into the head—and life!—of the rock star I was the first time, which is what I really want. If I have to move to a different dimension, *that's* the one I want to be in. I don't even care that he wasn't (or isn't) very happy. He just didn't appreciate what he had. If I were him, I'd be a lot happier. I'd *make* him happy.

Even though I'm not thrilled about the reason for it, I eat my stew quickly. I would definitely have preferred to savor the food, despite my hunger. When I'm finished, I look up at Luna, who's seated across from me.

-Does it ever stop?

She doesn't have to ask what I'm referring to.

-Not so far.

-But you...you're a spinner too, right? I don't see you falling on the floor and drooling like a zombie, off in some alternate dimension for an hour.

-No, you don't.

Her face becomes grave, her green eyes losing some of their glint.

-You're the only one who spins this much, Eon. That's why you're unique.

-So far.

Circe gestures at us with his dripping spoon.

-We're just starting here, man. There will be more of us.

-Someday.

Luna agrees.

-But we don't know when. In the meantime, Eon, you're the one who gives us the best chance of finding...someplace...safe. And when you do, other revolvers will be found and Atropos will make the bridge. We'll be able to start all over again.

-And not fuck up so bad.

Circe adds.

-Exactly.

I sit back in my chair.

-But, why? Why do I spin so much?

-Think of it as your destiny.

We all turn to see Atropos in the doorway. She has snuck up on us yet again.

-Destiny?

Circe snorts, as is his custom.

-There's no such thing as destiny, Atropos. There's alive and there's dead. I'm here because I want to stay alive and I don't give a shit where that happens. I want to be alive and as comfortable as possible.

Atropos slowly walks around the table towards Circe and I'm half hoping she's going to give him the Vulcan grip or karate chop his head off, but she only places a hand on his shoulder.

-With any luck, you will be. It's what we all hope for, isn't it?

I'm anxious to hear his reply—this is an interesting conversation—but unfortunately, I miss it, spinning away into the ether.

## CHAPTER TWENTY-TWO—The Bartender

Sennacherib's is swamped with people tonight. Even by a regular Saturday night's standards, it's busy and Hoop and I work the bar like magicians, almost dancing around each other as we grab different bottles from the shelves on the wall behind us and snatch cash from outstretched hands waving bills like flags of surrender.

I have to admit, it's a bit of a rush. Doing what you're naturally good at makes it all the more enjoyable and while I might not be able to wield an axe like Ace Frehley or whip out a novel like Kerouac, I'm a fucking wizard when it comes to slinging drinks and offering up service with a smile. The tips I get bear this out but, as fun as this is and everything, I'm looking forward to the end of the night and waking up tomorrow to go car shopping with my best girl, Daisy.

The fucking jalopy I've driven into the ground for the last six years needs an upgrade and I'm going new. Not new to me new, but *new*. New car smell. I can't fucking wait.

I notice Harvey sauntering in, but pretend I don't, moving quickly to the other side of the bar. Let Hoop deal with him. Ever since I got clean, his attitude towards me has been shitty. He acts like he's my wife and caught me fucking around on him. Always tossing me dirty looks and snide comments. I'm not in the mood to deal with it tonight. I'm feeling good and I'm not about to let his petty bullshit ruin it.

Out of the corner of my eye, I see Harvey pushing his way through the crowd, following me down the bar, making it pretty obvious it's me he's after but then I see a blonde dressed in black leather and I'll be damned if everything else doesn't just fade into the background for a few seconds. Even the juke, blaring something by that shitty punk band Green is the Enemy, has its volume reduced by half as I watch her approach the bar, hips swinging.

I glance over at Hoop and notice him noticing her and think, figures. Hoop is pretty smooth with the ladies and knowing him, he'd steal her out from under me anyway, even if I did stand a chance with a chick like that. Hell, if I even attempt to talk to her, he's liable to run and tell Daisy on me, playing it off like a joke, but she'd be pissed and he'd secretly be pretty fucking happy with himself. To say we've been down this same road before would be an understatement.

A red haired guy with a Mohawk bangs on the bar with the side of his fist.

-Another round over here, man!

-You got it.

I reach into the cooler beneath the bar and bring up two dripping bottles of Andromeda for him. When I look up again, the blonde woman is standing beside the redhead and Harvey is coming up behind her.

I hand the guy his beers and meet her eyes.

-What can I get for you?

She leans over the bar and almost shouts to be heard.

-How about five minutes of your time?

I'm pretty sure I must have heard her wrong and so, I lean in towards her, meeting her halfway across the bar.

-What's that?

-I asked if I could have five minutes of your time.

Yep. Definitely heard it right the first time. I look at her more closely, thinking she must be yanking my chain—someone put her up to this shit—but her green eyes show not a bit of humor. Which doesn't necessarily mean anything other than she's good at keeping a straight face.

I hesitate for only the briefest of moments, look over at Hoop, whose attention I don't even need to get as he's already looking this way and flash him a five signal. He nods and turns back to the thirsty crowd.

When I get to the other side of the bar, the blonde presses her lips to my ear.

-Outside, okay?

-Sure.

Harvey tries to grab me as I pass him, but I shake him off and keep following the woman in leather.

Once we're outside, I wish I'd remembered to grab my jacket but that's the only complaint I can come up with. This woman is gorgeous and, yeah, I'll admit, I have a little sex fantasy pop into my head. Beautiful stranger dragging me into the alley next to the bar to unzip my jeans and kneel before me, just begging for it.

But it doesn't happen.

Instead, she asks an odd question.

-Do you know me?

I look at her and I'm sure she can tell I'm pretty puzzled.

-Excuse me?

-Do you know me? Do I seem…familiar to you?

-Uh…

I feel like she's given me free reign to look her up and down, which I do, with pleasure. I try not to focus too long on her body but dragging my gaze to her face again proves to be more difficult than I would have expected.

-I don't think so, no. should I?

She shakes her head and looks past me.

-I guess not. It's just that…

Trailing off, she shifts her weight from one foot to the other.

-Just that what?

-Never mind. I'll just sound like a complete lunatic.

I laugh but quickly bite it back when I see she isn't amused in the slightest.

-Lunatic?

She shakes her head again.

-I guess it is funny only because of my name. Luna.

Her green eyes search my face, I think, for a sign of recognition.

-That's a pretty name.

-Doesn't ring a bell though?

I pause, thinking about it.

-No. Sorry. What is this about?

-Like I said, it'll sound nuts.

-I'm a bartender. I'm used to nuts.

She surprises me with a smile.

-It's just that…well, I've been dreaming about this place.

She gestures at the plate glass window with Sennacherib's name stenciled on it in fancy gold lettering.

-The bar?

Luna nods.

-The name of it. How it looks, both inside and out. And…you. I've dreamed about you.

I'm taken aback but try not to show it too much.

-Really?

-Yeah, that's why I think we must know each other somehow. But, I just can't remember where we've met before. I've been having the dream for weeks and I've watched this place from across the street a few times. Saw you coming and going. I thought it would jar my memory to see you, but when it didn't I figured, what the hell. Just ask him, you know? So, that's what I'm doing. But…

She sighs and tucks a long strand of blonde hair behind an ear.

-I guess not.

I notice Harvey watching us from inside the bar, which doesn't make me at all anxious to get back to work even though it's damn cold out here.

Instead, I try to make Luna feel better.

-Well, you've been here before, haven't you? At some point? I mean, everyone's been here at some point. This place has been around forever. And I've been hanging out here for years. Long before I started working here. We've probably crossed paths before and just don't remember it.

-No. I've never been here, except, like I said, to check it out. I never come to this part of the city.

So much for that theory.

-Well, not sure what to tell you then. I still think you must have seen me somewhere. Maybe just walking down the street. Who knows, right? Dreams are funny that way.

She nods, but I get the feeling her mind has wandered away. Maybe she *is* just a crazy person, after all.

I clear my throat.

-I guess if there's nothing else, I should get back to work. Packed house tonight.

-There is one more thing.

-Yeah?

-Do you know a black girl with blondish dreads and really pale blue eyes?

-Uh…

I don't just pretend to think about it, I really do.

-Not that I can recall. Why?

-She's in my dreams too. Both of you. But there's no place in particular. I mean, with you, there's this bar, but when it's the three of us, we're just in a room together. Like, a fancy room in a big house. It has a fireplace and burgundy furniture. Does that sound familiar?

I shake my head.

-I've never been in a fancy house in my life. Sorry.

She looks more than just disappointed. I'd say she looks totally crushed. I try to cheer her up.

-Hey, maybe it's something from a movie? I dream about shit I've seen in movies before.

-I don't think so. It's driving me crazy.

I try to give her my most sympathetic look, but I'm not completely sure how to give one of those and hope I'm not grimacing.

-I really should get back inside.

-Okay. You must be freezing.

-Yeah, pretty much. It was…uh…nice meeting you.

-You too.

I start back to the bar's door.

-Eon?

-Yeah?

I glance at her.

-You didn't tell me your name.

I'm not positive, but I think she might be right.

Her eyes go a shade of sad.

-Pretty good guess on my part, isn't it?

Wrapping my arms around myself, I nod.

-It's a damn good guess.

-Still think I'm nuts?

-I didn't say—

-You didn't have to. I saw it on your face. But it's okay. I'd think I was nuts too.

-I really didn't though. Like I said, I just think dreams are weird and we don't understand them.

-Okay. There is one more thing though. That guy?

She lifts her chin toward the bar window and when I look, Harvey is still there, still watching.

-Watch out for him, Eon. He's not a friend.

I chew my lower lip for a moment.

-You know him?

-I've never seen him before in my life. Not my waking life at least.

-Right.

-I have a feeling we'll see each other again.

I'm not sure if that's good or bad but I smile just the same.

-I hope so.

-You might change your mind when it happens.

She turns away and walks off down the sidewalk and I watch her go with a twinge of regret I don't understand. When she turns the corner, I go back inside and now I'm looking at Harvey a little differently. I don't view him as just a sleazy pain in the ass anymore so much as a predator—a cat—and I am most definitely his favorite toy                                                        mouse.

## CHAPTER TWENTY-THREE—The Junkie (12)

This is ridiculous.

None of this makes a single iota of sense anymore. I sit in my assigned room and stare out the window. Night is falling, as it always seems to be lately. Daylight is only a memory—one that's fading fast. The sun seems to be receding, as though it's found a preferable place in space to hang out and give life to more worthy beings than those of us crawling across the surface of the murdered blue planet.

Fuck the sun and fuck this place.

I'm tired of it. I don't want any part of this shit anymore.

I quit.

When I told the others about my last spin—how I met an alternate version of Luna who had no idea what the fuck was going on, and neither did I—the alternate version of me, I mean—they all decided to have a meeting and excluded me. Told me to go to my room, of all fucking things. What am I, seven?

This is bullshit.

I'm beginning to think I'm just as much a prisoner as Hoop is. Would they let me just walk out of here? Or would those big dudes with the guns block my way?

For all I know, this could be exactly what happened to Hoop. Maybe he had second thoughts about this shit too.

And then there's Halleck.

Where does he fit in? How did he even come across Satellite?

I'm beginning to wonder if any of this shit is even real.

What if Satellite, as I suspected before, really is just a hallucinogen? Maybe the spins are just what I thought they were in the beginning: regular, old trips. Or just dreams.

Which brings me back to Luna.

If she's so special in this bizarre hierarchy, then why doesn't the alternate her know what's happening? *That* version of her was either fucking with *that* version of me or...or what?

Atropos is supposedly not even human, therefore there's only one version of her. At least that was my understanding.

Watching the indigo sky deepen to black, I know I have to get out of here. Especially if these people—if they're people at all—intend on keeping me in the dark.

I get up from the chair and go to the door, expecting it to be locked from the outside, but the knob turns easily in my hand and when I poke my head into the hallway, it's surprisingly deserted. I for sure thought one of the armed guards would be standing watch over me.

Making my way down the hall, I pay attention to the oil portraits decorating the wall between the golden glowing sconces. All the paintings appear to be of people from bygone eras. The eighteen hundreds at the latest, a few men sporting handlebar mustaches but mostly women wearing bonnets, all of them as grim as funeral attendees.

When I reach the top of the stairs, my luck runs out. Circe is climbing them and sees me right away.

-Where you going, Eon?

I stop and debate a moment. Do I play it cool or just try to barrel past him and hope he doesn't kick my ass or pull a gun on me.

-Nowhere. Just getting hungry.

He reaches the top and stops next to me.

-And curious?

I shrug, hoping I seem indifferent.

-Let me give you a piece of advice, little man.

Circe puts an arm around my shoulder, which I'm definitely not comfortable with but allow it anyway. For the moment.

-What's that, Circe?

-If Atropos tells you to wait in your room, she has a good reason and you should wait in your fucking room.

Now I shake the arm off me.

-That's bullshit. She's only, what? Seventeen?

-You have something against teenagers? Think they're not as smart as you?

-Oh, is this the part where you tell me she's not human and so has wisdom beyond all of us combined? Because to tell you the truth, fuck that. Do I look like I was born yesterday?

Circe leans against the banister and smiles.

-You're getting feisty, there, little man. What put a fire in your belly? Was it being told to go to your room while the rest of us have a private talk? You insecure about what we might be saying—or *not* saying—about you?

I glare at him, my hands balling into fists at my side.

-There's a method to her madness, Eon. She doesn't want your brain tainted.

-What?

-It's the truth. If you go spinning off into the stratosphere with certain knowledge in your head, it could be dangerous for everyone.

-Everyone? Who the fuck is everyone?

He makes a face.

-You have trouble with vocabulary, man? Everyone. As in, *everyone*. The whole fucking planet.

I hate repeating myself, but I do anyway.

-Bullshit.

-You think this is a game? We're not fucking around here, man. Atropos knows what's coming and if we don't get out of here soon, we're all fucked. And that little spin you just took? Meeting Luna, who *clearly* knew something was up? That just proves we're running out of time.

I'm not usually a demanding guy, but my patience is wearing thin.

-How does that prove anything? Why the hell don't you guys tell me what's going on? Maybe I can help.

-You're helping already, man. You're the revolver.

-Circe!

We both turn to see Atropos and Luna coming up the stairs. Circe mutters a curse under his breath and runs a hand over his balding head.

-You said it was time to tell him, Atropos.

Circe sounds like a whiny little kid now, about to say it's someone else's fault he stole the cookies from the jar.

Atropos's eyes blaze with blue fire.

-I will tell him what needs to be done and in the appropriate manner. It is not your job.

I decide to intervene on Circe's behalf, which probably surprises me even more than it does him.

-Hey, at least he's being honest with me. Not sending me to me to my room like I'm a child.

When Atropos reaches the top of the stairs, she turns her gaze to me and she doesn't look happy.

-It is not my intention to treat you like a child, Mr. Eon. It is for your own protection.

-Protection from what?

There is a moment when I don't think she's going to answer. She's just going to leave me hanging. But then she does.

-From yourself, essentially.

-Oh? How do you figure? Is this the whole *oh, he's just a stupid junkie* thing because I may be a junkie but I'm not stupid.

-No one thinks you're stupid, Mr. Eon.

I look at all their faces in turn and they are all equally expressionless.

-Then why don't you tell me what's going on? What's the revolver?

Atropos shoots a nasty glance at Circe again before replying.

-It's exactly what it sounds like. You will revolve us all into an alternate dimension.

I must be looking at her like she's insane because that's when Luna speaks up.

-Think of it this way: a revolver—a pistol—has a cylinder, right?

-Yeah, so?

-That's why it's called a revolver. It revolves to the next chamber. It goes around and around and that is basically what you've been doing.

-But a revolver only has six chambers. I've spun more than six times. For the analogy to work, I should have already gone back to the rock star.

Circe speaks up in his same snide tone.

-Way to be anal, dude.

-I'm just saying.

Atropos explains further.

-In theory, this is how we believe the spinning works. But we already know there are an infinite number of dimensions. We would have to spin an infinite number of times to have a repeat visit to one of them.

I'm getting totally lost and I hate being lost.

-Then what's the point? Even if we find a perfect

dimension, we'll never be able to get back to it.

-Not until we find the trigger.

-The *trigger*? Oh, come on! Give me a fucking break here!

-I know there is a trigger, but not who or what it is. Because you spin more frequently than anyone else, you're the one who is most likely to be able to find the trigger before it's too late.

-Too late? It's already too late.

I know I'm starting to be belligerent but I don't care. I want this over with.

-It will be soon enough but trust me, we don't want to be here when it happens.

-What?

Raising my voice, I throw my arms into the air with frustration. Both Luna and Circe step closer to my side, as if ready to tackle me if the need arises.

-What's gonna happen? Nuclear war? Alien invasion? A plague? Tell me!

-Does it matter?

Atropos is not the slightest bit intimidated by my outburst. Her voice is still smooth and calm and if I were a betting man I'd say her pulse hasn't increased even the smallest fraction.

-I don't know! Maybe it matters. Maybe it's something I could survive.

-Maybe it is. It's highly improbable but perhaps you could. But what about the rest of the world? Do you not care what happens to everyone and everything else?

My first instinct is to shout *you're damn right I don't care* but I stop myself because, am I really that much of an asshole? Thinking about it, I don't believe I am. Yes, I've done some shitty things but at my core, I *do* care and Atropos knows it. I can tell by the way she's looking at

me. In fact, I think Circe and Luna know it too.
 I say the only thing I really can:
 -Fuck!

## CHAPTER TWENTY-FOUR—The Deputy

The town of Bellflower is a far cry from the city where I grew up and I wish I'd moved here sooner. Better late than never, of course, but it probably would have spared me a lot of grief in the long run.

The main thing I find here that I never found anywhere else is kindness. Also, the folks in this place have a mutual respect for one another that city people tend to be lacking. Back there, no one gives a crap about anyone else, but here, people will actually go out of their way to help a friend or neighbor in need.

Hell, even a stranger, which is what I was when I first arrived. I was a drunk with no assets to speak of. No skills. Just a desire to get away from the people who wanted to keep me down and wanted me to accept my station in life.

I'm not sure what gave me the strength to finally look around and say I want out, but it wasn't the love of a good woman or a fear of death or anything else you're likely to find as a motivation for a hero's journey in a book or movie.

Not that I'm a hero. Not by a long shot. I'm just a man who tried to be a good person and I guess it was ultimately that desire that got my feet moving and landed me here in small town America with nothing but a duffle bag of clothes and a beat-up pick-up truck.

I'd just been driving, no destination in mind. But I knew I wanted the country, I wanted fresh air and lots of tall trees generations old and the sound of birds in the morning. Not pigeons either.

I'd been driving for two days when I stopped in Bellflower's diner for some pie and coffee and I just never left. I knew it almost immediately. This was the place. I could heal here and I did.

At first I got a job in that very same diner-Sam's-working as a fry cook, then I moved on to the lumber mill and finally, after making friends with sheriff Patrick Roberts, he, having more faith in me than I'd ever had in myself, hired me on as a deputy. It was a part time gig until I proved my mettle and took some college courses over in Indigo Bend, but now I'm full time and pretty much Pat's right hand man.

Carol, the waitress at Sam's Diner, is bringing me another cup of coffee, her cottony white hair almost making her look angelic somehow, dazzling in the sunlight.

-Let me guess. You want another refill?

I grin at her.

-Now that you mention it.

As she's filling my mug, she returns the smile.

-I don't know how you can consume so much caffeine, Jeff. I'd be nervous as a cat full of rocking chairs.

-I couldn't function without it. Well, it and candy. And sugary cereals.

She laughs and moves away to the next table where old Joe Macintyre is sitting and reading the paper.

It's somewhat miraculous, but they still have newspapers in this town. It's like living with a bunch of luddites but in the best way possible.

I check my watch and see it's nearing five pm. Another day with nothing doing. And it being a Tuesday night, I expect more of the same. Most of the people in this town are early to bed, early to rise. There are exceptions of course. Mostly the town drunks and teenagers, but they rarely ever get up to anything more than rowdiness.

Popping the last bite of pecan pie into my mouth, I look out the diner's window and see a long black car pulling into the lot off the highway. Not one I recognize but Route 55 is the main drag through town, winding off to other, bigger, places in both directions, so people pulling in as they pass through is nothing unusual.

I pull some bills out of my wallet and toss them onto the table top, downing my new cup of coffee in three long gulps.

While I'm standing up and putting my hat back on, the person driving the car walks into the diner and I do a double take.

It's Halleck.

Immediately, I feel my blood temperature rise a couple degrees and I'm tempted to pull the brim of my hat down and avert my gaze as I pass him on the way out. But, that would do no good. He's looking directly at me and his face isn't showing a single lick of surprise. He expected to find me here.

He saunters up and stops at the table I'm still standing beside.

-Hello, Eon.

I cast a quick look around the diner. Old Joe has glanced up from his paper, watching me with interest but Carol is busy at the counter. Sam is back in the kitchen and no one else is in the place. It'll fill up soon though. Lots of townies like to come here for dinner. Sam makes the best damn meatloaf in four counties.

-What are you doing here?

I keep my voice low.

He smiles the way I'd imagine a snake would smile if it

could.

-That's no way to greet an old friend, *Jeff.* Where are your manners? I've heard you're a respectable man nowadays. I'd have figured you'd be polite.

I ignore the histrionics and repeat the question.

-What are you doing here?

His smile broadens.

-Came to see you, of course. May we sit? Maybe have a cup of coffee?

-I have to get back to work.

I start to walk past him but he grabs my forearm, stopping me.

-I think you're going to want to listen to what I have to say, *Jeff.*

Yanking my arm free, I lower my voice even more.

-Don't touch me again.

He gives a little bow of his head.

-My apologies, Deputy.

The title makes him snigger and my anger rises a bit closer to the surface.

-But, please. Let us have a quick chat. It won't be more than five minutes of your time. I promise.

I start walking again, my back to him and suddenly a loud crack explodes in the diner and I whirl around just in time to see old Joe collapse face first into his paper, the back of his head sporting a new, wide, wet, gleaming hole and the booth behind him splattered with brains and gore.

-Now that I have your attention, Eon, may we sit and speak a spell?

Halleck is holding a smoking .45 and I pull my .38 from its holster and shout at him.

-Drop your fucking weapon *now!*

I'm dimly aware of Carol screaming but it sounds far

away. I dare a quick glance in the direction of the counter and see her frozen there, two mugs in each hand.

I yell at her to get down, but have to repeat it twice before she snaps out of her trance and does as commanded.

Halleck speaks just as casually as ever.

-I'll kill her too, Eon. Just as easily as I blew out the brains of the old timer there. And anyone else who happens to come in. Not to mention the fat old chef who's peeking out at us right now.

He directs his attention towards the kitchen and yells.

-*Peek-a-boo, I see you!*

-Whatever this is, leave them out of it!

When he looks back at me, his expression is one of amusement.

-That's up to you, Eon. We could have been having a nice cup of coffee right now but you had to go and be difficult and rude about it and now that gentleman right there has gone to meet his maker. And all because you chose to be a snotty little prick who forgets where he came from.

-What the fuck are you talking about?

-Drop your weapon, Deputy.

He must be joking.

I don't even lower it, never mind drop it.

-No way.

Halleck fires in the direction of the kitchen. Something explodes back there—ceramic mugs, probably—and Sam lets out a yelp. One of pain or fear, I can't tell.

-You're practically glowing.

Halleck tells me, smirking again.

-Did you know that? You're like a pregnant woman. Just glowing away. Or like a candle flame and all the little moths, myself included, are drawn to you now. You'll never be able to hide again.

-I don't know what the fuck you're talking about and I don't give a shit. You put down the gun or I'll be forced to shoot you. You have until the count of three.

I pause, waiting for his trigger finger to so much as twitch, but it doesn't.

-One.

-Two, three. I don't care about your counting, Eon. You're a good guy now, remember? You won't shoot me. You'll arrest me, certainly, and probably give me a good beating to go along with it, but shoot me? I doubt it.

I fire my gun, shooting him in the thigh. He drops, screaming, and fires his own weapon into the ceiling before swinging it back in my direction.

Diving into a booth, I swear I can hear the sound of the bullet passing over me, right where my head previously was.

Halleck shrieks with fury.

-*I will own you, Eon. Do you understand? I will fucking own you and that will be the end of all this. You will never escape, no matter where in the universe you try to hide.*

He fires his weapon repeatedly in my general vicinity, but the old red vinyl booth proves to be suitable protection.

I get on my radio, calling the sheriff, telling him to come quick. There's a known drug dealer in the diner. He's already killed one person and has attempted to murder both myself and others in the building. He's clearly on some kind of drug, but I don't know which one.

Hurry.

# CHAPTER TWENTY-FIVE—The Junkie (13)

When I tell the others what Halleck said, Luna and Circe exchange worried glances with each other. Not Atropos though. She doesn't seem worried so much as surprised.

-What does it mean?

I ask the question like a child asking about God.

Luna is the first to reply.

-He's taking Satellite for one thing.

Atropos agrees.

-He's taking it and is fully aware of what's happening. He was able to completely take over his alternate self.

Chiming in, Circe says,

-That dude is gonna wonder what the fuck is going on once Halleck comes back from the spin.

We're all in the dining room. Again or still? I don't know anymore. Time has become such a fluid, flexible thing. And not just time either, but also space. Even the space in my head is not to be trusted anymore.

-He said I was glowing. Like a flame. And others would be able to find me now. And he didn't make it sound like it was going to be a good time for me. Well, the other me. Or *me's*. Whatever.

-Yes.

Atropos's voice is thoughtful.

-You're becoming more powerful, which does give you a certain aura which will cross with you through dimensions. I'm curious as to how he found you so quickly though. This last spin of yours was one of the shortest you've had.

-Then he's aware.

I can't tell if Luna is angry or scared when she speaks.

-Aware or awake. Maybe both.

-He must be the trigger.

Watching the two women converse is like watching a tennis match without knowing the rules of the game. I am, as I always have been, lost at sea.

-Wait a minute.

Circe holds up a hand.

-Halleck can't be the trigger. If he was, Hoop would have said so.

Luna comes back quickly.

-Did you ask him?

-Well, no, but—

-Then we should.

Getting up from the table, Luna pulls a hair band out of her front hip pocket and pulls her hair back into a tight ponytail. I suspect this is a sign she means business.

-Let's do it!

Circe pounds the table with an enthusiastic fist and also gets to his feet.

-You coming Atropos?

She doesn't answer, obviously lost in thought. I speak up instead.

-I'm coming too.

Luna shrugs and Circe mimics the gesture.

-Fine by me, little man. I mean, since you two are buddies and all.

-We're not buddies. We haven't been buddies in a long time.

-What about in that universe where you were so happy to be slinging drinks with him? Sounds like you were buddies then.

-Yeah, well, not in this lifetime. Not anymore. The

dickhead had me tied up in his fucking basement, remember?

-The night we met? How could I forget? It was so romantic. Luna had to rescue you.

He blows a kiss at me and I feel like leaping over the table and choking the snide out of him. Instead, I decide to be the bigger man and ignore his stupid ass.

Since Atropos doesn't protest, the three of us go upstairs and Luna pulls out an old fashioned key and unlocks the door to the library where Hoop is being held.

He's asleep on a leather sofa when we enter, a plaid red and blue wool blanket thrown over his lower body, his head resting on the sofa's arm.

-Rise and shine, cupcake!

Circe practically yells the words, startling not only Hoop, who comes awake with a small cry of alarm, but also myself. Luna only sighs.

Sitting up straight, Hoop whips the blanket off his body as if he's pretending to be a matador flipping his cape. He swings himself off the couch and charges Circe, leaping over a huge oak coffee table in the process.

With barely any physical motion at all, Luna shoots her fist out, catching Hoop in the throat easily. He goes down gagging.

Circe starts laughing and I have to admit, it's tempting to join him, but I'm too busy being impressed with Luna's self-defense skills to be too amused.

-You have to teach me how to do that.

She gives me a little smile that makes my heart flutter like a damn school girl's, then she bends over and questions Hoop.

-Why didn't you tell us Halleck is the trigger?

He coughs, holding his throat, then croaks out a curse at her.

-Fucking bitch.

This makes Circe laugh even harder.

-Uh oh, Luna. He called you a bad word.

-Yeah, I heard him.

She takes a step towards Hoop and I expect her to kick the shit out of him but she walks around him and sits down on the sofa, tossing the wool blanket over the back.

-What do you think of the library, Eon?

Not knowing what her game is, or even if she's playing a game, I take the room in. It's just as impressive as the rest of the house and it definitely lives up to its name. All four walls contain floor to ceiling bookcases that appear to be just as old as their contents, which seem very old indeed. In addition to the sofa, there are several forest green stuffed plush chairs and two massive intricately carved mahogany desks, each with matching sturdy chairs. The room's accents are silver and in the few places the walls are visible, a green and silver diamond pattern wallpaper reminds me of what I imagine an old casino might look like.

-It's nice.

-So many books to read.

Luna talks casually, as if she didn't just drop a dude with at least sixty pounds on her.

-But I bet Hoop hasn't spent his time in here wisely. Have you, Hoop? Did you partake of all the wisdom that can be found in these old tomes?

-Go fuck yourself.

Circe *tsks*.

-That's just rude, man.

Luna crosses her legs and continues.

-What can you tell us about Halleck, Hoop? He's taking Satellite. We know that much. What else is there?

Hoop folds himself into a sitting position on the floor

and continues to rub his throat.

-I have no idea what you're talking about, Kat.

My eyes shift over to Luna, who has no reaction, so I decide to be adventurous.

-Kat?

Luna absently swings a booted foot up and down.

-My real name is Kathleen. I used to go by Kat.

-Huh.

This is interesting information, I think.

-So, then…why Luna?

-It's the name Atropos gave me.

-Oh. I see.

I don't really see, of course. I think it's weird. Like Atropos is her mother or something.

Circe elbows me.

-Bet you can't guess my real name.

I think about it.

-Cock gobbler?

He gives me a fake grin.

-Funny. You're a funny guy.

-Okay, I give up. What's your real name?

-I'm not gonna tell you now. Asshole.

-Whatever. Did Atropos name you too?

-Yep. She gives nicknames to all of us who are worthy. Not dickless though.

He points at Hoop and whispers to me.

-If she gave him one, it would probably be Vag.

I frown.

-How come I don't get a nickname?

-You're obviously not worthy, little man.

Circe snickers, happy with himself.

-Or maybe I'm higher up the ladder than you. Maybe only peons get nicknames.

A quiet knock on the doorjamb alerts us all and we

turn to see Atropos standing in the doorway. I'm starting to think she does this kind of thing a lot.

Her blue eyes find mine.

-Your name is Ringer.

I blink.

-Huh?

Even though I apparently *am* worthy of a nickname, I'm not worthy of any further response. She comes into the room and looks down at Hoop.

-What do you know about the trigger?

He tries to play it tough but I'm pretty sure I see fear in those brown eyes.

-I don't know anything about it.

-You know what I can do to you if you don't cooperate. What I can do *with* you.

This threat puzzles me for a moment, but then I remember her somehow jumping into Hoop's body and making him walk up to this very room. Just the idea of someone else controlling my body like that gives me the willies.

Atropos continues talking in her calm voice.

-I can dig around in your mind until I find it myself, but the chances are very high if I do that, your mind will become irreparably...scrambled. I have no desire to hurt you. You know this.

To my shock and amazement, Hoop begins to cry, pressing a fist to his mouth and using the other hand to wipe away the fast forming tears.

Atropos crouches down beside him.

-You can rejoin the fold whenever you wish. You know this too.

Circe scratches his neck and says exactly what I'm thinking.

-He *can?*

Without taking her eyes off Hoop, Atropos replies.

-Of course he can. He was brought into it to begin with for the same reasons you all were. For your potential to repair what's about to go very wrong.

Licking my lips, I glance over at Luna, who seems fully engrossed in what Atropos is saying. I wonder again if I've inadvertently gotten involved in some kind of cult. Their devotion to this strangely beautiful teenager is unlike anything I've ever witnessed before, and that includes a junkie's devotion to his or her drug of choice.

Hoop sniffles loudly, wiping his nose on his sleeve.

-Halleck developed something else. Another drug. A *better* drug. He calls it *Sol*.

Silence permeates the room, all of us too stunned to speak. Finally, Atropos asks Hoop a question.

-And this new drug does what I can do?

Hoop nods and continues to sob.

Rising up, Atropos regards us all gravely.

-There can be no more tests. We have to go now.

Confused, I say,

-What? *We?* Where do we have to go?

Without missing a beat, Atropos replies.

-Wherever you're taking us next.

## CHAPTER TWENTY-SIX—The Guard

I never held a gun before I got this job and I pray to whoever there is to pray to that I never have to pull the trigger. But the money is good and being out in the middle of nowhere is helpful to my mental health.

The blonde woman, Luna, recruited me right off the street one day when I was hanging around waiting for Sennacherib's to open. Just walked up and asked me if I wanted a job. I was skeptical at first but when she told me what they were paying and that it was a live in gig, I bit back my better judgement and crossed my fingers I wasn't going to be fed to some millionaire with an excessive appetite for man flesh.

She taught me how to use the AK and how to be alert. Those were her words: *be alert*. See anything out of the ordinary and just take aim. Questions would have to come later.

I'm outside on gate duty, freezing my balls off with another dude named Dylan, on a Tuesday night and everything is as calm and quiet as a tomb. Dylan offers me his pack of smokes, but I shake my head. Yet another vice I gave up a long time ago. The *longest* ago. I quit the cancer sticks before the drugs and even before the alcohol. I thought I'd live longer, as much of a joke as it sounds like now.

Something rustles in the bushes and Dylan freezes, his zippo ready to set his long hair on fire.

-Cat.

I try to stifle a smile. Dylan's greener than me. He lights his smoke and snaps the zippo closed, pocketing it fast so both hands can be on his weapon again, the cigarette clamped tightly between his lips.

-Lots of cats around here.

I'm hoping he'll stop being quite so jumpy.

-Which is good on account of the rat infestation.

He pulls the smoke from his mouth.

-The fuck? I hate fucking rats.

I shrug.

-They're not that big. Don't sweat it.

-I had a rat chase my dog once. I tried telling Penguin it was supposed to be the other way around. He was supposed to chase the rat, but he was the biggest pussy dog on the planet. Great Dane. Scared of his own shadow.

I give him a sidelong glance.

-You named your dog Penguin?

-Yeah. So what?

Unable to help it, I crack up. It's not all that funny, really, but not much is funny anymore and I take the laughs wherever I can find them.

The sound of clacking footsteps coming up behind us makes me choke on my laughter and both Dylan and I whirl, weapons ready.

Three people are walking towards us through the dark, coming down the walkway from the house. If it wasn't for Luna's blonde hair, I might have been further alarmed.

-Easy, boys.

The voice drifts to us, masculine and somehow taunting. I know the voice. It's that douchebag Circe.

The three of them reach us: Luna, Circe and Hoop. The last guy I only know by sight and name. I've never had a single conversation with him before now but he is the one to speak.

-Take a break, Dylan.

Dylan doesn't question it and I have to admit I'm kind of envious of his type. The kind who just take orders without question. He would have been a good soldier probably. Me—not so much.

When Dylan is out of earshot, Luna tells me something I'm not expecting to hear.

-We need to talk to you about Atropos.

I don't say anything. I've heard of Atropos—I know she's the reason we're all here—but I've never met her. In fact, most of the other guys I'm working this gig with have never met her either. We've never even seen her. There's been talk that maybe she doesn't exist. Not as a person anyway. Maybe she's something else. A code name for something. A secret project maybe. The damn house is so big, they could be doing anything in there and those of us on the 'staff' would never be the wiser. We're only allowed in rooms on the first floor. We can go to the second floor but we're always made to stand outside doors, never allowed inside rooms.

-How would you like to meet Atropos, Eon?

The question comes from Hoop, his bald head gleaming in the frozen moonlight.

-Meet her? What for?

-It's better if she tells you that.

-But there is one thing.

Luna speaks again, her voice low and sexy, and I'm reminded of the first time I met her in front of the bar. How I'd hoped she was just stopping to talk because she dug how I looked, because I sure as shit dug how she looked. Still do.

-What is it?

-You've heard of the drug Satellite?

I'm slow to answer.

-Yeah…
-You've done it?

No sense to lie.

-A couple times, yeah.
-Well, we need you to do it a couple more.
-What? Why?

Hoop says again,
-It's better if Atropos tells you.
-Why is that?
-Because you won't believe it if you hear it from us.
-Come on, little man.

Circe reaches for my arm but I take a step back.
-I'm not supposed to leave the gate.
-Dylan will be right back.
-I'm not supposed to leave it for *anything*.
-You can leave it for us,

Luna says.
-But it will be unmanned.
-Tell you what.

Hoop gives Circe a gentle push forward.
-Circe will stay here until Dylan gets back.

Circe glares at him in the dark.
-Oh, I will?

I interrupt them.
-He doesn't have a weapon.

Pulling out an automatic, Circe waves it at me.
-Trust me. I have a weapon.

I can't think of anymore arguments, so I just nod and follow them to the house, leaving Circe behind to grumble to himself.

Once we're in the house, Luna and Hoop lead me into the parlor where an old woman sits waiting.

She smiles at me, her skin so translucent I can see the blue veins spidering their way through her temples. Her chocolate brown eyes regard me with curiosity as she rises to her feet.

-Hello, Mr. Eon. I'm Atropos.

She offers her hand and I take it. It feels like I'm holding a bird's skeleton. I didn't expect her to be so old.

-Hi. Nice to meet you, ma'am.

-Sit down, will you? Join me for a cup of tea?

She looks at Hoop who immediately leaves the room, presumably to fetch the tea.

I do as asked and sit down in an arm chair across from the sofa where Atropos sits.

-You're a very special man, Mr. Eon. Very unique. Did you know that?

-Uh...no. But...umm...thank you.

I have no idea how to respond to this situation. I'm not used to being around old ladies. There's just not as many of them as there used to be.

-You're about to become even more unique.

I shift in my chair.

-Oh?

Is she going to offer me a promotion or something? To be her personal bodyguard? No, it can't be that. She has Luna and Hoop and Circe for that. And besides, I'm not a tough guy. If anything, I'm more apt to run away than stay and fight.

-That's not true at all.

I snap back out of my thoughts.

-Excuse me?

-You're not more apt to run, Mr. Eon. You think so little of yourself but it's not true. You have within you the capacity for true heroism.

Licking my lips, I'm wishing the tea would get here already. I'm suddenly incredibly thirsty. *Did she just read my mind?*

Atropos smiles kindly.

-I most certainly did. And I can do even more than that, Mr. Eon. I can see your heart.

-My...heart?

-Oh, yes. I can see your courage. Of which you have more than enough to get the job done, I can assure you.

I'm starting to feel a bit spacy. Not an entirely unpleasant feeling but I think I need to keep my wits about me now, so it's not the most welcome thing in the world either.

-I'm sorry, ma'am—

-Please call me Atropos.

-Sorry. Okay. Um. I'm sorry, Atropos, but I have no idea what you're talking about.

Her smile spreads further.

-Not here you don't but elsewhere you do.

-Excuse me?

-In an alternate dimension.

I stare at her.

-We're here because of your glow.

-My *what?*

-Hoop, Circe, Luna and myself. We followed your glow. I admit I had to do a bit of the steering to get us all here in one piece, but we don't have time to go into that right now. What we have to do is give you more Satellite.

I have no idea what this crazy old chick is talking about but I know one thing for sure: I need to get the fuck out of this house full of whack-a-doos and funhouse mirrors.

-Not yet.

Atropos's smile wanes the slightest bit.

-How are you doing that?

-Reading your mind?

-Yeah. Why do you even have to ask?

-I've found it makes people feel a little better if I feign ignorance every so often. Freaks them out just a tiny bit less.

To that, I have no response.

Hoop enters the room carrying a silver tray with a teapot and cups with saucers.

Atropos's smile returns.

-You can quench your thirst now, Mr. Eon. And by doing so understanding will come to you. Of course, you won't be here when it does, but that's a whole other matter you needn't concern yourself with.

Hoop pours tea into one of the cups and hands it to me. It's drugged. I know this as sure as I know my own name. But I know one other thing as well. I know that whatever is happening here is exactly what's supposed to be happening and I know it because Atropos is telling me so. Her voice is in my head and it's the most comforting thing I've ever heard. So I drink.

## CHAPTER TWENTY-SEVEN—The Junkie (14)

The first thing I ask when I come out of it this time is if Atropos can read minds.

It seems like a silly question when I say it out loud, but being violated in such a way trumps feeling silly.

-Sometimes.

Is the answer Luna gives me.

-Like when?

-When she's at her strongest.

Impatiently:

-Which is when?

-Are you being dense on purpose? This is the least of our worries.

I suppose she's right. But I'm beginning to wonder what's real. I was just, after all, in this same room with almost all of the same people. Hoop and Atropos aren't here at the moment but I can hear voices in the next room, which means they were either just here or are about to be here.

Probably.

-We were all together. In the spin.

Luna nods.

-Yes.

-But that alternate me...

I trail off, not knowing what I want to say.

-Had yet to be initiated.

She offers.

Circe is over by the windows, peering out at the night from between the curtains.

-I'm starting to wonder which one of me is real.

-All of you. All of *us* are real, regardless of which dimension we're in. How could you not know that by now?

I don't have time to answer. Atropos and Hoop enter the room and I'm surprised to see them holding hands.

-Atropos...

I'm not sure what I want to say to her. Something about her staying out of my head, but I'm also curious about the *other* her. The old white woman who oozed kindness while *this* version, while kind enough, lacks...shall we say...warmth?

-Why are you the only who isn't the same?

I finally put one of my thoughts forward.

-That seemed like a fine dimension, didn't it?

She has chosen to ignore my question and is addressing everyone as a group, asking her own.

Circe turns away from the window.

-As good as any other, I guess.

-We need to make a decision. Luna?

Luna remains silent, but thoughtful for what is probably close to a minute. Finally, she speaks in a soft voice, more gentle than her usual one.

-I don't know. We just don't know enough about it. We never left the mansion.

-But we were *there*. We know what our alternate selves know. I sensed no fear. No urgency. Did you?

-No, but...we were in a secure mansion.

Atropos changes the subject.

-We need to keep Ringer safe.

There's a long moment where I'm frowning. Ringer? And then I remember. She's not calling me Mr. Eon anymore. Not here anyway.

I fiddle with the cuff of my sleeve, buttoning then unbuttoning it.

-Because of my...uh...glow?

-Precisely. I can sense it even now. You're no longer safe here. I suspect others will be arriving soon.

-Others?

-If we can go to them, then obviously they can come to us. And they will.

-But, why?

-To destroy you. You're the revolver.

-But I haven't found the trigger. Halleck. Wouldn't *that* be of more interest to them?

-They don't want you to find it, Eon.

Luna looks guilty for a second.

-I'm sorry. *Ringer.*

I don't care about the slip. I doubt I'll ever be Ringer in my own head anyway.

From across the room, Circe speaks up.

-You *can't* find it. If you find it and use it, the cylinder will spin and one world will be used up, shot off into nonexistence.

All three of us look at Circe as if he's lost his mind, but he's already pulling out a gun. I blink in confusion at the round black eye of the muzzle as it swings towards me. It all happens in slow motion, just like in the movies. There's a flash of light and a deafening bang and the upper part of my arm seems to disintegrate in a red mist and I'm knocked off balance, as though a truck just plowed into my left side. I hit the floor hard and Atropos is suddenly on top of me, shielding my body and above us there's more explosions and yelling, but it sounds muffled and faraway. Atropos yells something in my face but I don't think it's English or any other language I've ever heard.

The commotion happening in the room is disorienting and I realize I'm terrified, almost certainly about to be killed and I don't even know why.

*This has happened before.*

Over and over again, we do the same things, never realizing how alike we all are. Not just a little alike, but exactly alike, no matter what our labels or social standings. We are only creatures, like so many other creatures, repeating the same routines again and again and again.

There is no beginning and no end.

*I* am the revolver and *I* am the trigger.

This is how it was always going to be, how it was meant to be. There never was any other choice.

Reaching up with my good arm—I try to use my other arm as well, but I can't get it to work at all—I place my hand against Atropos's temple and our eyes meet.

Neither of us are afraid anymore.

We spin.

The room we're in, whirling, blurring by in a cacophony of colors and shapes. Nothing is solid. Nothing is liquid. Not even us. We are both *in* space and *are* space, rotating end over end, twirling in and out of time, *here* one instant, *there* the next.

All the dimensions—all the lives—are one and the same and they roll through us and us through them, like blood through the veins of the universe.

## CHAPTER TWENTY-EIGHT—The Host

Inside the mansion, I greet the guests one by one, offering a handshake or a cheek kiss, depending on gender, and always a wide, welcoming smile.

There are close to thirty people here now, with more scheduled to arrive. There is champagne and other beverages, anything a person could want, at the open bar in the ballroom, not to mention more hors d'oeuvres than I care to name. This is not a dinner party though, so hopefully people have come with their bellies already full.

This is a celebration, though most of the people here are unaware of that fact. They've been invited with no knowledge of why, asked to come however they feel comfortable, but to be aware a stretch limo will be picking them up and delivering them here at eight o'clock sharp.

Frankly, I'm surprised so many of them showed up. I would have been too suspicious, myself. If I'd had a gold-embossed engraved invitation hand delivered to me as I was just going about my day? I would have assumed a prank at the least, and something secret and sinister being even more likely.

But they've come and though some of them wear expressions of confusion, they seem happy enough to drink and explore the house. Some have even been brave enough to mingle, striking up conversations with one another and whispering—*What could we be here for?*

I'm dressed in a tuxedo for the first time in my life. Maybe the last. It doesn't feel right. It's as though I'm wearing a disguise and I suppose I am. The disguise of a secret savior? Maybe. Like one of my own childhood heroes, Mr. Bruce Wayne himself. Because everyone knows Bruce was Batman's mask and not the other way around.

Likening myself to a hero makes me feel like a pompous ass though. As if I planned it and worked for it and deserve it. None of those things are true. All of it was an accident. Atropos says it's true but even Atropos can be wrong sometimes. I don't know why I was chosen. Maybe it was all the drugs, the apathy. The just not giving a fuck. But whatever it was, I'm grateful for it.

Luna sidles up next to me, a glass of white wine in her hand. She looks stunning in a satin topaz blue dress that shimmers, her blonde hair piled atop her head and pinned in place with an ornate silver clip. She's wearing makeup for the first time since I've known her and I have to admit, it's my least favorite part of her look tonight.

She links her free arm with mine and sips her wine, observing the guests with bright eyes.

Even though it's not obvious, I suspect she's wearing a holster somewhere, probably on her thigh, and there's something about that secret knowledge I find incredibly sexy.

Her voice is smoky and low.

-Enjoying yourself?

I keep my voice down.

-Not so much. This isn't really my idea of a good time.

-Look at the bright side. You're not being forced into a damn dress and heels. What happens if I need to run in these things?

-Kick them off?

-Hmm. You were supposed to say 'you won't need to do any running tonight.'

-I was? Okay, sorry. You won't need to do any

running tonight.

After a moment's thought, I add,

-And hopefully no shooting or ass kicking either.

She gives me a sideward glance.

-I've done enough of that for now.

I believe her and wish she didn't have to do more but I have a feeling she will. The war—Halleck's war to keep people here, on this world, and enslaved to his drugs—may only be the beginning. Every dimension we've been to, he is the same or close enough that the difference is not worth noting.

Atropos says this is statistically impossible; we are bound to find a home where Satellite and Sol don't exist. At least, not at the time we get there. And if we can get to him before he meets the one genius chemist, we might just find ourselves with a good place to finally cease our endless spinning. Atropos says we will and when we do, we'll be able to stop. She will see to it.

I don't know what that means, what it entails, but I believe her. She has powers greater than any of the rest of us can understand.

An old, white woman crosses the front door's threshold and strides up to Luna and myself with purpose, a playful smile playing at the corner of her mouth. Her brown eyes twinkle beneath the light thrown down by the chandelier above us.

-Hello, again, Mr. Eon.

I nod and return the smile, though I'm somewhat confused.

-It's Ringer now, actually.

-Oh, I know.

The woman, in a sparkling green evening gown decorated with hundreds of sequins, looks around at the gathered group of people.

-You're expecting more, I take it?

Luna is the one who answers.

-We are. Many more. The night is still young.

-That it is,

the woman agrees.

I can't keep the question back any longer and I blurt it out, barely quiet enough to keep anyone nearby from hearing.

-How are you here? I mean, you're also over there.

I point to the other side of the room where Atropos— *our* Atropos—sits chatting with someone I don't recognize. A middle-aged Asian woman.

-We, and I, have our, and my, ways.

Luna and I clutch each other just the tiniest bit harder.

The old woman smiles again, with a kindness which seems otherworldly in its honesty. Kindness like that, that can be sensed rather than seen, just doesn't exist in this world. Not often, anyway. But I'm getting used to it and even manage a genuine smile in return.

Atropos touches my free arm, the one not gripped by Luna.

-Are you ready to give your speech?

I stare at her for a moment, waiting for a punch line, but none comes.

-What? *Me?*

-You, Mr. Eon.

-But…I don't know anything! How can I make a speech?

-You can and even beyond that, you *must.*

I look at Luna.

-She's joking, right?

Luna appears to be quite mystified as well, but shrugs.

I see a mischievous twinkle in Atropos's eyes as she moves towards a table and helps herself to a glass of champagne and a fork to tap it with.

-Oh, god, no.

Instantly, I feel sweat seeping from my armpits, collecting beneath my balls, dampening my palms.

Atropos walks back to us with her weapons of choice, still smiling.

-Are you ready?

-No! I'm *not* ready! Please, Atropos, don't make me do this.

-You'll be fine.

I let go of Luna, thinking about fleeing, but where would I go? Upstairs? Outside?

Much to my horror, Atropos taps the glass with the fork, drawing everyone's attention.

-Ladies and gentlemen, thank you for coming. I'm sure you're all wondering why you're here. I can assure you there is a very good reason. This planet is all but finished. We all know this. But tonight you're going to discover a solution to this problem. A way out. The way has been tried and proven to be quite successful...

Atropos continued talking for a while more, but I was too stressed to listen. Why *me*? Why did she want *me* to tell them about this 'way out?'

A voice in my head spoke then, unmistakably mine but so much calmer than my usual voice, amazingly self-assured, confident and unwavering.

-*You're the revolver. Everyone senses something special about you, even if you don't sense it within yourself. You have power and a unique talent. They will both listen and believe. They will trust you, just as the Spinners do. You will not steer them wrong. The world will be new again, worth saving and fighting for. Have faith. We're waiting for you.*

I felt my spine straighten then, knowing another me was somewhere close, holding out a hand, not the slightest bit frightened, and that knowledge made me brave.

Atropos was introducing me now and everyone's gaze was on me. I had no idea what I would say to them, but felt confident it would be the right thing.

I cleared my throat, smiled, nodded to each face in turn, and then began.

-*Don't eat animals.*

I said.

-*Recycle.*

-*Drive an eco-friendly car. Or better yet, don't drive at all. Walk. Or bike.*

-*Leave only footprints.*

-*These were, quite literally, the signs of the time, once upon a time...*

I talked for a while and no one snickered, no one rolled their eyes. They listened, just as Atropos knew they would.

When I thought I was finished, the people still watched me expectantly and I felt compelled to add just a little more.

-*None of us ever knows how close we are always coming to the brink of extinction and disaster. Every moment we're only a hair's breadth from total annihilation. Decimating extinction. Every second of your life, you just dodged another bullet.*

-*Virtually everything you've ever been, good or bad, you can be again. You can steer your life in any direction you choose. Towards the horizon or away from it. Left, right. Up, down, diagonally. You can turn your life inside out if you want to and a lot of people do. Every single day, people are making the choice to begin again. Start over. Do the right thing.*

-*Imagine the possibilities. We're like space, limitless and constantly expanding. Freedom to choose is a luxury we in this room have. All we have to do is not fuck up too bad.*

Some of the people laughed at that. Some nodded in understanding. Everyone, I think, understood.

So did I and the others save the world? Maybe for a moment. We can all save, or at least *change*, the world for at least a moment. It's not very hard once you know how. You too can be a world revolver.

Spin.

Revolve.

*Evolve.*